The airboats roared through the swamp, searching for him

Mack Bolan palmed a hand grenade, released the safety pin and let it sink somewhere between his feet, another contribution to the swamp. The bottom feeders couldn't eat it, but if the Executioner's plan worked out, they would have food aplenty in the next few minutes—meat enough to gorge themselves for days.

And if he lost, then he would feed the swamp himself. No one escaped the food chain in the end. He had a chance this night, but it was only that: no more, no less. If he survived, the credit would be due to skill and luck in equal parts. And where did fate come in?

He put the question out of mind and concentrated on the spotlights, bearing down on him from the south.

MACK BOLAN ®

The Executioner

DON PENDLETON'S
EXECUTIONER®
ZERO TOLERANCE

A GOLD EAGLE BOOK FROM
WORLDWIDE.

TORONTO • NEW YORK • LONDON
AMSTERDAM • PARIS • SYDNEY • HAMBURG
STOCKHOLM • ATHENS • TOKYO • MILAN
MADRID • WARSAW • BUDAPEST • AUCKLAND

First edition January 1998
ISBN 0-373-64229-6

Special thanks and acknowledgment to
Mike Newton for his contribution to this work.

ZERO TOLERANCE

The essence of evil is the abuse of a sentient being, a being that can feel pain. It is the pain that matters. Evil is grasped by the mind immediately and immediately felt by the emotions; it is sensed as hurt deliberately inflicted. The existence of evil requires no further proof.

—Jeffery Burton Russell

Fear succeeds crime—it is its punishment.

—Voltaire

It's time to let the evil men experience a little pain and fear, receive their share of punishment.

—Mack Bolan

To all the victims of oppression and terror in the Caribbean states of siege. Keep fighting.

PROLOGUE

The smell of incense woke Ferris Burke, and he nearly gagged on the pungent fumes that seemed to get inside his head and fill his sinuses until his skull felt close to bursting.

The DEA agent's whole body seemed to hurt from the beating he had taken when they grabbed him, something like a sap or metal pipe impacting on his skull with force enough to put him down and out.

Burke had absorbed at least a dozen kicks and punches prior to that, of course, when he was still in shape to fight. There was no telling how long they had kicked and beaten him when he was down, unable to resist. They had a score to settle, and he would have been a total fool to look for mercy now that he was in their hands.

Shit happened, man.

He almost laughed aloud at that, but there was too much pain, and now he was thinking of his partner, Tom Carlisle. If they had blown *his* cover, what about the rest of it?

The bastards had to know something, or he wouldn't be tied up like a Christmas turkey waiting for the oven. Still, that didn't mean they knew it all. His partner could be in the clear, for all he knew, which meant they would be after information, would stop at nothing to extract the data from his head before he died.

Burke turned his head from side to side, a painful exercise, and tried to figure out exactly where he was. It was some kind of rustic building, larger than a shed and smaller than a warehouse, with a smell of animals behind the incense.

There was another smell about the place, beneath the incense and the barnyard odor, something he should recognize, if he was thinking clearly. His thoughts were still a little scrambled, and he felt a strange reluctance to identify the odor. He knew he'd hate it when he worked out the puzzle, so he avoided the solution while he bent his thoughts to other problems.

Getting up, for instance.

He was dizzy from the pain of the beating he had taken, but it wasn't hurt that kept him stretched out on his back. His arms and legs were bound, spread-eagle, on some kind of heavy wooden table. Rope that had the greasy feel of nylon was looped around his wrists and ankles, tight enough that he could barely move. The effort cost him, even so, with waves of fresh pain crashing on the inside of his skull.

The undercover agent closed his eyes, tried not to lose it in the sudden dizziness. It would have been a simple thing to just let go, pass out, but he was worried that his time was running out, that he might not wake up again.

No, that was wrong.

If all they wanted was to kill him, he would already be dead. They could have crushed his skull or shot him, left him where he fell or dumped him in the nearest bayou as an appetizer for the alligators. Bringing him to this place, wherever the hell it was, meant that they wanted him alive...at least for now.

Burke cherished no illusion that his enemies would have a sudden change of heart and let him go. Whatever they were looking for, revenge or information, there was no escape clause in the contract. They would kill him if he let them, and right now, it didn't seem that he would have much choice.

There was his partner, granted, but a one-man rescue

would be dicey, and the very thought assumed that Carlisle was still alive. If they had overlooked his partner somehow, there was no good reason to believe that Carlisle would even know he had been lifted. They'd been out of touch, deliberately, the past ten days to minimize the risk of being seen together, picked up on a wiretap, anything at all. Unless Burke's partner went back on their deal, he wouldn't even try to get in touch for two more days.

And Carlisle was a pro. He followed rules, unless he had some damned compelling reason to ignore SOP.

Carlisle would come if he knew there was trouble, but he couldn't know, unless *they* knew...in which case he was dead.

Burke caught himself before the panic could take hold and start him thrashing uselessly against the nylon ropes. If he could work out how the bastards had seen through his cover, there was still a chance that he could talk them out of killing him. Mistakes were made sometimes. There might be explanations for suspicious circumstances, if he only had the time to think about it, work out something in his mind.

Still, given any kind of choice at all, he would have opted for a free hand and a loaded gun.

Burke had been eight months on the job with Carlisle, playing both ends off against the middle, out of touch with everyone but their control, and barely hanging on to contact there, because the stakes were too damned high if someone blew it. Fourteen years with DEA, and he had spent eleven of them working undercover, one gig or another, polishing his skills until he was the best around.

Well, maybe second best.

He never could have worked this sting, if not for Tom Carlisle. Setting up a buy was one thing, but they needed someone on the inside, nice and close, if they had any hope at all for a clean sweep. Between the two of them, he was convinced they could have pulled it off.

So, what went wrong?

The question haunted Burke, the more so since he had no ready answer for it. There was nothing he could put his finger on that would explain how it had gone to hell. No faces from his past to burn him, no false moves or careless words that he could think of. Even when meeting Carlisle, he had taken special pains to watch for shadows, anything at all that would have indicated they were blown.

There had been nothing. Nothing he could see.

But here he was, spread-eagle on the table like...like what? The incense worried him, and even so, it took another moment for his mind to click on the connection.

He wasn't lying on a table. He was stretched out on an altar!

Desperately he threw his weight against the ropes once more, but there was no play in the knots, and his position gave him little in the way of leverage. He finally gave it up, knew it was best to save his strength and put his thoughts in order, try to plan a line of bullshit he could sell to save himself.

He heard a scraping sound and identified it as the kind of noise a wooden door would make on dirt as someone dragged it open. Footsteps drew closer, coming from the general direction of his feet. It was an effort not to crane his neck and look, but he wasn't about to show them he was worried. Not if he could help it.

He counted half a dozen of them, standing back some distance from the altar, watching him. They had their shirts off, wearing low-slung jeans or baggy trousers, barefoot on the dirt floor of the barn. Their sweat-slick upper bodies had been marked with abstract patterns, drawn in white and red, some kind of paint that didn't run.

He recognized Philippe Bouchet and Louis Germaine, but the rest were strangers, tall and short, a range of skin tones, some with frizzy hair, a couple wearing dreadlocks. He figured, nothing ventured...

"You, Philippe, what is this shit?"

From the far end of the barn, beyond his line of sight, a set of bongos started thumping, an erratic beat that set his teeth on edge. He was about to ask Bouchet another question when he saw the others turn and stare at someone moving toward them from the general direction of the drummers. Seconds later, two more figures moved into his field of vision, dancing to the jerky, syncopated beat.

And what a pair they made.

The woman was stark naked, her body glistening with sweat or oil, her hips and firm breasts thrusting to the rhythm, moving like a finely tuned machine. In other circumstances, she would certainly have turned him on, but in the present situation, he could only stare, distracted by the flapping, squawking chicken that dangled by its feet from her left hand.

The woman's partner banished any latent traces of eroticism that remained in the performance. Tall and muscular, he wore a battered top hat and a long frock coat, with dusty-looking trousers underneath. His face was painted ghostly white to simulate a skull. Around his neck, a live, thick-bodied snake, some six or seven feet in length, was wriggling to the music, its forked tongue flicking in and out to taste the incense-laden air.

Burke almost broke then, knowing what it had to mean, but there was still a measure of control remaining as he raised his voice, competing with the drumbeats.

"Hey, Philippe! My man! You're making a mistake here. I don't know who you've been talking to, but—"

Skull-face leaned in close and slapped him, hard, across the face. Burke was smart enough to recognize a warning, and he didn't push his luck. Provoking them right now would only make things worse. As long as they were dancing, he was relatively safe. Unless he missed his guess, things would start getting hairy when the floor show ended.

Maybe he would have another chance to plead his case, throw out some sort of story that would make them hesitate.

Or maybe there would be a miracle.

Right now, he needed one.

He almost missed it when Germaine produced a long, slim-bladed knife and passed it to the naked woman, who was dancing past him. She was in some kind of frenzy now, her body swiveling and jerking as if she were plugged in to a generator, current flowing through her limbs and torso. It was quite a show, but Burke was mostly focused on the blade, more than a little apprehensive as she sliced the air with sweeping strokes. Skull-face avoided her, his dark eyes watchful, handling the snake like it was nothing, dancing to the drumbeats with a death's-head grin etched on his face.

The undercover agent had a fair idea of what was coming—fair enough to make his stomach roll, his scrotum shrivel—but it still surprised him when the naked woman moved in close and held the chicken something like a foot above his upturned face. The knife flashed, blurring through a single, practiced stroke, and something struck his forehead, bouncing out of range. His mind made a connection to the chicken's severed head, but then a crimson shower hit him in the face, and he was focused on not breathing, trying not to inhale chicken blood.

It didn't last that long, in real-world time. Burke knew when it was over, since the warm rain stopped, and he could hear the woman move away, her bare feet shuffling in the dirt as she retreated. Opening his eyes, he had to blink away a stinging scarlet veil. The sharp, metallic smell of blood was in his nostrils, nauseating, but he damned well had to breathe.

Skull-face was still in sight but barely moving now, his feet shifting slightly to the drumbeat, while he mostly stood there, watching. On the captive's left, the others moved in closer, swaying to the rough percussion rhythm, like fascinated spectators at some sporting event.

Or students in an operating theater.

He tried to sound aggressive, righteously pissed-off, with no fear in his voice. "Yo, man, Philippe! This shit has gone on long enough! I don't know what your problem is, but—"

"*Damballah!*"

Philippe Bouchet's shout echoed in the barn, making any protests utterly superfluous. Burke didn't know what Bouchet was saying as he started spouting more words in an unfamiliar language, but the gist of it was clear.

The feces was about to hit the fan.

He strained against the nylon ropes once more, unclear on what he planned to do if they should snap, but it wasn't a problem. He was trapped, without a hope of breaking free unless somebody cut his bonds.

As if in answer to his thoughts, Bouchet produced a long, straight dagger from behind his back. He raised the knife in both hands, tip pointed at the rafters of the barn, and launched into some kind of chanting diatribe that could have been a sermon or a really miserable song. Burke understood that he was running out of time and made a final bid to save himself.

"We need to talk this over, man!" he said. "I'm telling you, this is a serious mistake! The guys I work for aren't about to let this kind of shit go by, you hear me? I came down here in good faith, to do some business, and you're asking for a war we both know you can't win!"

Bouchet ignored him, started working on the buttons of his shirt. The knife was razor sharp, the barest touch enough to sever threads and fibers. In another moment, he was naked to the waist. Skull-face edged closer, standing on his right-hand side, the others on his left.

They all had ringside seats.

Burke felt himself begin to hyperventilate. He couldn't

help it. All the times he had faced death in stings and drug burns, raids and drive-by shootings, it had never been like this. He'd always had a chance before, at least to fight to save himself. The helpless feeling he endured now was worse than simple fear. The impotence he felt enraged him and it robbed him of his manhood, all at once.

Germaine and his companions had begun to chant along with Bouchet, lifting their voices in a kind of ragged chorus, drumbeats muttering behind them in a sultry undertone. Skull-face leaned closer, grinning through his war paint, while the boa wrapped around his neck remained the most aloof observer of the lot.

"Goddammit, this is wrong!"

Of course, they knew that going in, but it was all that he could think of now, his bullshit arguments exhausted at the moment of his death. There was no syndicate to help him out, much less avenge his death. Carlisle would have a fair idea of what went down, more so if he was found.

It was bizarre what flashed into your mind as you were checking out. No wife or kids at home to think about, and they could mail his pension to the NRA, for all he cared. Tears stung Burke's eyes, and he could feel the blood rush to his face as he began to curse his captors, using every verb, adverb and adjective he had acquired in thirty-seven years of living, blistering their ears.

As if they gave a damn.

Bouchet reversed the knife and smiled.

The prisoner had time to scream once, putting everything he had behind it, as the blade came flashing down.

1

The water moccasin was four feet long and thick around the middle, sluggish looking even in the face of danger. In the darkness, it could easily have blended with the lumpy cypress knees where it lay coiled, until it shifted at the larger predator's approach. The viper's sturdy neck curved in an S-shape as it poised to strike, the jaws agape to bare the snowy-colored flesh inside that gave the deadly snake its common nickname.

Cottonmouth.

Mack Bolan knew the snake could strike a full third of its length from solid ground, no sweat, and from the present perch, it might go airborne without meaning to. He held the sound-suppressed Beretta steady, preferring not to fire as he gave the moccasin a wide berth, water swirling sluggishly around his knees. The mud sucked at his feet but didn't slow him appreciably. He was careful not to lose his balance, knowing that a heavy splash could ruin everything.

He hadn't come this far to give himself away through simple negligence.

The cottonmouth was well behind him now, no threat, although its mouth was still wide open, baring inch-long fangs that packed a lethal punch. Out here, an hour's heavy slogging from the highway, any bite that reached a major vein or artery would be a death sentence. He might survive the hemorrhaging induced in fleshy tissue by the viper's hemotoxic venom, but the odds would be against him, either way.

In fact, the odds were all against him now.

He holstered the Beretta, reached back for the Colt Commando slung across his shoulder, muzzle down, and concentrated on his destination. It should be another hundred yards or so before he reached the bayou camp where Doobie Arnold took delivery on his shit. The trousers of his tiger-stripe fatigues were soaked through to the skin from wading, but he barely felt the stagnant water on his skin. Mosquitoes hummed around him, but the war paint he had used to darken face and hands kept most of them at bay.

Another fifteen minutes or so remained before his target was in sight.

He had considered boating in, using a black inflatable designed specifically for such amphibious maneuvers, but he would have needed extra time to make his way along the bayou's twisting watercourse, instead of hiking overland. There *was* dry land around—or spongy land, at least—but he had left the last of it behind some fifteen minutes earlier as he started wading on the last lap of his journey.

Almost there.

The really tough part, Bolan knew, would be getting back.

It was impossible for him to know how many hardmen would be stationed at the camp. They were expecting a delivery the following night, and while he could have waited, tried to catch them with the merchandise, he had decided it would serve his purpose just as well to raze the camp before the coke arrived. His information was that Doobie Arnold had been forced to front a full third of the money to satisfy his man from Medellín. Whatever happened to the shipment, whether the Colombians backed out or simply held delivery for a later date, the bayou boys would be out a quarter of a million dollars.

He heard a splash upstream behind him and immediately froze. There was a chance that they had sentries posted out this far to watch the camp, although it seemed unlikely. Drifting closer to the mangroves, watching out for snakes, he turned and trained the automatic rifle in the direction he had come from. Nothing moved, aside from the slow ripples spreading on the surface of the brackish water.

Bolan waited long enough to satisfy himself that no one was pursuing him. An alligator would attack from underwater, and there was nothing he could do to guard against it, short of calling off the strike.

He held the light assault rifle ready and started to move back downstream. If there was something stalking him, it wasn't human, and he couldn't see it in the dappled shadows of the swamp.

His boots stirred up the bed of algae underfoot, and pungent gas from rotting vegetation filled his nostrils. Bolan breathed through his mouth, ignoring it, dismissing any thought of flukes or leeches from his mind, concentrating instead on the shadows that could hide a human enemy.

On balance, though, he didn't think his enemies would have guards posted far outside the campground. Doobie Arnold had been operating from the bayous nearly unopposed for six or seven years, and even now, with trouble on his hands, smart money said that he would trust the swamp as his first line of defense. Most of the killing had so far been done around New Orleans, Baton Rouge and New Iberia, on urban battlegrounds.

Until tonight.

The bayou boys were watching out for certain adversaries, but they hadn't reckoned on a visit from the Executioner.

He heard the enemy before he saw them, voices raised in ribald conversation, with a generator panting in the background. If they were concerned about an ambush in the middle of the night, it didn't show from their behavior.

Bolan took advantage of the ruckus, moving closer, watching out for any stray security devices Arnold's soldiers might have planted in the mangroves. He was betting they would shy away from high-tech gear, especially in a setting where exposure to the elements and prowling animals would make frequent replacements a necessity.

As luck would have it, he was right.

Now all he had to do was scope the campsite, find a weak point and move in.

THE WORST THING about bayou pickup duty, Dwight Carnes decided, was the bugs. Mosquitoes, biting flies and such would eat a man alive if he wasn't careful. Suck the blood right out of you like tiny vampires, giving you diseases that would knock you on your ass and right out of the game.

Carnes always sprayed himself with bug repellent any time he had to work the bayous. Used a full can, going in, and never mind the way it made his shirt stick to him like a clammy layer of sweat or suntan oil. One thing nobody ever called ol' Dwight Carnes was a fashion hound. T-shirts and jeans were good for everyday wear, maybe a denim jacket if the nights got cool or it was raining. On the rare occasions when he had to dress up for a meeting, maybe catch a funeral or something, he wore any one of half a dozen Western shirts he kept at home for dolling up.

It didn't help that much, of course, but there was only so much he could do about his looks.

The cheap cigar between his teeth had gone out twenty minutes earlier, but Carnes liked to chew them as well as smoke them. Better, sometimes, since the stogies didn't make him cough until he lit them up.

He listened to his men gassing, Eddie Fletcher talking shit about how good he was in bed and how the women always begged for more, the kind of nonsense no one who had ever seen him in the shower would believe. The others ragged him long enough to make Eddie mad, but that was fine. He wouldn't fight about that kind of crap unless he had been drinking hard, and Carnes kept it down to three, four beers apiece when they were on a job.

Like now.

He knew the shipment wasn't coming in until the following day, and it might be late at that, but Doobie Arnold had insisted that they stake out the delivery site a day ahead, make sure no one was waiting for them, setting up a double cross.

These days, when Arnold spoke of trouble, he meant Haitians. They were giving him a fit around New Orleans, even up to Baton Rouge, and cutting in on business something fierce. It should have been an easy job to root them out, but they were tougher, somehow, than the local blacks Carnes had grown up with. Damned Haitians, with their mumbo jumbo from the islands, didn't have the sense to know they were outnumbered and outgunned. They acted like they thought they had a chance.

But they had never trespassed on the bayou country.

Never yet.

First time for everything, of course, but it was hard for Carnes to believe that anyone could be that stupid, coming after Doobie Arnold's men and merchandise out on the bayou.

He was sitting out here with his men, though, in case somebody did. It wasn't Haitians that Arnold had in mind this time, but rather the Colombians who were delivering a major load of flake. Colombians were slippery, and they would cut your freakin' throat for fifteen cents, much less to grab a million dollars on a deal that let them keep the flake, besides. A double cross was definitely possible, and while the boys from Medellín had never tried to sour any of the deals before, there was a chance they had been waiting, biding their time, until a fat-assed payday came along.

So Carnes kept his Mini-14 rifle handy, making sure the others didn't wander off somewhere and leave their guns behind, not even for a minute. If there *was* an ambush coming, it was possible the other side would try to sneak some people in ahead of time, which helped explain why Carnes and his men were in the swamp a whole day early, complaining about their mosquito bites and waiting for the Indians to make it snow.

And that was why he had the reinforcements coming in.

They wouldn't be arriving for a while, and that was fine, just so he knew the boys were on their way, enough of them to make the difference in a stand-up fight. Let the damned Colombians bring all the men they wanted to, if it came down to that.

He went to get himself another beer, was just about to crack it open when all hell broke loose. First, you had the boys relaxing, sipping brew, then came a burst of automatic gunfire from the north side of the camp, inland. The blast came right away, a couple seconds later, flattening the shack where Arnold had the radio installed. A ball of flame shot up, some thirty, forty feet above the camp, and Carnes heard somebody screaming out in pain.

He dropped the beer and clutched his automatic rifle, shouting in a hoarse voice as he ran back toward the scene of the explosion.

"Move it! *Move it!* Watch your asses, people! Find those fuckin' pricks!"

He didn't know how many were out there, and it only mattered when calculating odds. That didn't mean a thing to Dwight Carnes, right now. He knew that energy and guts were frequently enough to win a fight, regardless of the numbers. He had whipped three men at once, himself, and that was in a bar, bare knuckles. With the kind of hardware he and his men were packing, the attackers wouldn't stand a chance.

If they could find their enemies, Carnes thought, they could kill them.

Finding them at midnight on the bayou, though, could be a stone-cold bitch.

HE HAD THE FIRST CHARGE planted when it happened, no one's fault, the kind of unforeseen event that often turned the tide of battle, sometimes toppled kingdoms into dust and rubble. Bolan had approached the camp with every sense alert, on watch for roving sentries, but his targets were relaxing, drinking beer and cracking wise among themselves. Surprise was critical.

He took the northern shack because it was the closest, and because it had a shiny radio antenna poking skyward from the center of the roof. With a set like that, the smugglers would have had a shot at talking to Beijing. New Orleans would be child's play, and while reinforcements from the Crescent City would be too late to help his enemies, there might be other fighting units stationed closer to the bayou base camp.

He used C-4 plastique on the commo hut, enough to take it down without disorienting Mother Nature. Bolan didn't need a Hiroshima blast to do the job.

He was turning from the commo shack, prepared to wire a couple of the boats for doomsday, when he saw a gunner less than twenty feet away. The young man's fly was open, and his hands were full, about to bless the bayou with a little more effluvium, when he saw Bolan rising from the shadows like a demon from the swamp. He had a shotgun tucked beneath one arm, an awkward posture, but he did his best to reach it, opening his mouth to scream.

The Colt Commando stuttered, four rounds punching through the shooter's chest and vaulting him toward splashdown in the fetid water. Bolan hardly registered the kill, his mind already racing to examine options now that he had lost the critical advantage of surprise.

Worst-case scenario would be two dozen rednecks opening up on him, leaving his riddled carcass floating in the swamp. Confusion and too many beers prevented that from happening, however, and he had a few more heartbeats left before the hardmen could get organized.

He used that precious time to find himself a point he could defend, somewhere that offered a degree of shelter from incoming fire. While it meant he had to get his feet wet one more time, he counted that a minor inconvenience compared to death.

The dock where he had shot the sentry stood on wooden posts the size of sawed-off phone poles, painted black with tar or creosote, and driven deep into the muck below. The dock itself was made of metal, not unlike the landings on a fire escape. A person standing on the dock could look between his feet, therefore, and see the water underneath him, maybe watch an alligator or a snapping turtle pass.

It wasn't much, but it was cover of a sort. The metal would deflect incoming bullets—or at least he hoped it would—while Bolan found his combat stretch below his adversaries' line of sight.

Forget about the moccasins and leeches, rats and snappers. Nothing in the water was more dangerous than Doobie Arnold's soldiers, with their automatic weapons.

Bolan blew the C-4 as he slid into the water, felt the hot air of the shock wave buffet him and flatten his hair.

He hung on to the dock with one hand, chest-deep in the stagnant water, with the muddy bottom still a foot or so beneath his boots. If he let go, the water would be up around his nostrils, and he wouldn't have a view of anyone approaching him on foot. Right now, though, he was covered by the leaping, dancing shadows cast by the nearby fire.

He heard somebody shouting, rallying the troops, and several men sprinted toward him seconds later, each one carrying a long gun. Bolan let them close the distance to ten paces, sighting with his Colt Commando as they rushed toward him, hanging by his elbows from the rough edge of the dock. The sluggish current tugged at the Executioner's body, making him correct a fraction of an inch before he squeezed the trigger.

Half a dozen 5.56 mm tumblers caught the pointman in the chest and stomach, slamming him backward on the metal dock. The man behind him tried to leap across the fallen corpse, but Bolan's second burst reached out to meet him in midair. His body wobbled, tumbling as it fell, a loud splash marking impact with the water.

That left two, one of them charging on, while his companion stopped dead in his tracks and fired a submachine-gun burst that passed three feet over Bolan's head. The Colt Commando's muzzle-flash was giving him away, but there was nothing he could do about it at the moment, short of hanging on and fighting back.

He took the charging gunner first, on the assumption that proximity made him more dangerous. A 3-round burst sheared off the left side of the gunman's face and hammered him off stride. His legs turned into rubber, wobbling under him until he lost it and collapsed across the dock, blood streaming into the water through the rusty lattice-work. A short burst took out the surviving gunner.

He heard the airboats coming as the other shooters started closing in, the hoarse growl of their engines unmistakable despite the sharp, stacatto sounds of gunfire ringing in his ears. He couldn't tell how many of the big swamp buggies were approaching—two or three at least, if he was any judge of sound—but one of them could easily carry half a dozen men.

Which meant that it was time for him to cut and run.

It galled him, having to retreat before his enemies were fairly blooded, but the whole point of the exercise had been to shake them up, and not to sacrifice himself in the preliminary bout of his campaign.

He set down the Colt Commando and started disconnecting frag grenades from where they dangled on his combat harness. When he had four of the lethal eggs lined up in front of him, he started yanking pins and lobbing the bombs around the camp as quickly as he could, spaced so that they would detonate some thirty feet apart, along the rough edge of a semicircle forty yards across. Before the first one blew, he was retreating, pushing off into the water with his carbine hoisted overhead, backpedaling through mud that tried to suck his boots off, slowing progress to the pace of a slow-motion fever dream.

The airboats sounded as if they were right on top of him, then the first grenade went off. He turned back toward the bayou proper, running full out, heedless now of any wake he raised or noise he made.

Those who survived would soon be after him, and he was running out of time.

A COUPLE OF THE SHACKS were burning, and he had nine gunners dead or wounded, but the way it looked to Dwight Carnes, things could have been a whole lot worse. The reinforcements showing up just when they did had saved his bacon—for the moment, anyway, until he had to break the news to Arnold—and the main thing now was to get after those responsible and make their sorry asses pay.

He flagged down the nearest of the airboats, leaving Hector to console the wounded. It was Carnes's job to hold the fort, and that included giving chase to any hit-and-run guerrilla types who figured they could win a game of hide-and-seek against the bayou boys.

They were about to find out that it was the worst mistake they ever made.

He had to yell above the dull roar of the airboat's motor, leaning toward the driver on his high seat, while the buggy's huge fan sucked his words away. They understood each other, even so, and the driver nodded, waving him on board and giving orders over a walkie-talkie that connected him to pilots on the other boats.

Four hardmen waited for him on the airboat's wide, flat deck, all scooting over to make room for him as he came aboard. Carnes knew most of them at a glance, had worked with them before when Arnold had some dirty work that needed doing. They were cool heads, all of them, and seasoned killers. Anyone who tried to face them on their own home ground—or water, as it were—was in for a resounding disappointment.

"Let's go!" he shouted to the airboat's pilot, pointing at the bayou that would be his adversary's only angle of retreat. Whoever had shot up the camp, damned sure wasn't making out to sea, or else they would have passed the airboats coming in. They had to come from landward, and would double back the same way.

The airboats were equipped with spotlights, meant to help them navigate at night. In practice, they were often used for poaching gators, but they served for other game, as well. Mere seconds after takeoff from the camp, four white-hot beams of light were lancing through the midnight darkness of the bayou, crossing here and there like streams of tracer fire, sweeping out and back across the mossy trunks of cypress trees, low-lying hummocks, brackish waterways that came alive with red and yellow eyes.

The people Carnes was tracking, white or black, Colombian or whatever, were good enough to sneak up on the fishing camp and raise some hell, waste some of his boys before the reinforcements came and chased them off. That didn't make them bayou people, necessarily. Doobie Arnold paid the local Cajuns well enough to either help out with his business or else look the other way, and Carnes had no reason to believe that any of the locals would be fool enough to stab him in the back.

Not when they knew the punishment for treachery.

So his targets had to be strangers, and the timing of the

raid—within a day of the delivery from Medellín—was more than just a little bit suspicious. Carnes didn't reckon the Colombians were stupid enough to strike a day ahead of time, not knowing if the money would be in the camp. He calculated any double cross from that end would be sprung at the exchange—come in with big smiles on their faces and go out with choppers blazing, grab the money, keep the flake and run like hell.

No, simple logic told him this was someone else. The Haitians, maybe, or some other faction Carnes didn't even know about.

It would be nice if he could take a prisoner or two and grill them prior to filing his report with Arnold, but if they were forced to wipe out the bastards, so be it. They were dead men, anyway, once Arnold heard the kind of shit they had been pulling on his turf, the damage they inflicted on his men and property.

But Carnes had to find them first, and that was something else. Because the bayou was a deep, dark place in daylight; after sundown, it became the freakin' Twilight Zone.

It would be no great trick to miss one man, or even several, in the darkness, racing pell-mell in the airboats, with their spotlights burning through the night. No trick at all.

And if he let them get away, then Carnes knew he was as good as dead himself.

2

Time was elusive in the swamp, especially at night, when it couldn't be gauged by moving shadows. It was easy to lose track of time, and lose direction, too. The latter problem was resolved by Bolan's compass, which helped him maintain a course to the northeast. As for the element of time, he knew that it was running short when he heard airboat engines closing on him from behind, and saw their spotlights wobbling in the dark like giant fireflies, getting closer by the second.

Pausing long enough to count them, Bolan made it four. He couldn't picture any of the pilots coming after him alone, without some kind of backup, which meant odds of eight to one, at least. If they were running heavy, four or five men each, he could be facing up to twenty guns.

His options, on the other hand, came down to only two. He could attempt to hide and let them pass him by, or he could stand and fight.

It might not be that difficult to hide—one man in all that darkness, with the giant cypress trees, cattails and hummocks, so much water all around—but what would he have gained? He would be forced to play a grim, protracted game of hide-and-seek as he retreated to his vehicle, a long mile as the buzzard flies, but more than double that on foot. His progress would be slow, at best, but with the airboats hunting him...

So he would fight.

The enemy had him outnumbered, but the obvious advantage of their transport cut both ways. The swamp buggies were fast, all right, but they were also loud and bulky, handling much the same as any other motorboat. Their pilots couldn't put the airboats in reverse, for instance, neither could they follow Bolan on dry land. Their greatest disadvantage, though, was that he knew exactly where they were already, while the men behind the spotlights were still seeking him, with no idea whom they were looking for, how many men had struck the "fishing camp" or any of a dozen other variables that would have their nerves on edge.

He had perhaps a minute, maybe less, to choose his stand. The fat knees of a cypress, standing tall above the water, gave him cover, once he checked them with his flashlight, watching out for snakes. When he was huddled in the moldy-smelling niche, behind a drooping veil of Spanish moss, he fed the Colt Commando a fresh magazine and made a quick check of his arsenal.

Two frag grenades remained, which could cut the odds in two, if used judiciously. Five magazines remained for the carbine, thirty rounds in each, plus the Beretta 93-R and four extra magazines, each holding twenty rounds. The pistol had been drenched in stagnant water, but he counted on it to perform as needed. Rust wouldn't take hold for hours yet, by which time Bolan's confrontation with the hunters would be settled.

One way or another.

He could hear the airboats fairly roaring now, their spotlights burning through the pitch-black night. They were spread out across a front of sixty yards or so, two slightly forward of the others, in the middle, taking point. The way they had it covered, if he struck the leaders, men on one or both boats bringing up the rear would have a decent chance to spot him in the act.

He palmed a hand grenade, released the safety pin and let it sink somewhere between his feet. Another contribution to the swamp. The bottom-feeders couldn't eat it, but if Bolan's plan worked out, they would have food aplenty in the next few minutes, meat enough to gorge themselves for days.

And if he lost, then he would feed the swamp himself.

No one escaped the food chain, in the end.

"WE SHOULD OF FOUND somethin' by now!"

The pilot shrugged and concentrated on his driving, leaving Dwight Carnes to fume in silence. The camp was several hundred yards behind them, and he had been expecting contact with the opposition any second, ever since he climbed aboard the airboat. Now the empty darkness had him wondering if they had somehow missed their targets.

Was it possible?

Suppose the sneaky bastards had a speedboat waiting where they could reach it in a hurry if they had to? Carnes spit over the side and knew there had been nothing of the sort. That kind of motor, running in the swamp at night— they would have heard it even with the airboats growling.

Shit! Where were they, then? *Who* were they?

Going back to Doobie Arnold without answers was the next-best thing to suicide. Oh, it was doubtful he would actually be killed—though not impossible, by any means—but he would surely be humiliated, maybe have to take a beating from the pet gorillas Arnold kept around him like a palace guard. Carnes would be demoted; that was guaranteed. If Doobie kept him on the payroll, it would be some kind of flunky job that served as a reminder of his failure every day.

The one way he could salvage something from the whole mess was to round up the men responsible, dead or alive, and have some answers ready when he turned in his report. That way, when his boss started raging, Carnes could present him with a fair idea of who had tried to screw him while his back was turned. The wrath would fall where it belonged, on Arnold's enemies, instead of on his own loyal officer.

That was the plan, but so far, he was coming up with squat. Another hundred yards or so, and they would be beyond the point anybody could have reached on foot since the attack, no matter if the bastards walked on water.

"Wait! What's that?"

He pointed, shouting to the pilot, and the spotlight swung hard left in the direction he was pointing. Yellow eyes flared for a second, then the old bull alligator swished his tail and disappeared from sight, beneath the mucky surface of the water.

"I think we've come—"

Too far, he was about to say, before the other airboat blew. One second, they were running parallel, some fifty feet apart, and then there was a bang, like someone tossed a bowling ball into the buggy's giant fan. As Carnes turned to check it out, he saw the airboat bucking, lurching through a cloud of smoke and slowly keeling over on one side. A couple of the men on board were jumping for it, but he couldn't see the others, couldn't make out much of anything, in fact, except that spotlight, pointed straight up at the stars.

"What happened?"

Seated on the perch behind him, Carnes's pilot muttered, "How the hell would I know?" He was well beyond the wreckage of his sister ship by now. They had to turn and double back to check it out. The others, hanging back deliberately on either flank, were starting to converge, but cautiously, their spotlights dancing on the water, skittering among the cypress trees.

Hit something, Carnes told himself. Airboats were touchy that way, sometimes. You could drive one through the saw grass like a giant lawn mower, but it you hit a root or sunken log, next thing you knew, your ass was airborne. The explosion was a puzzler, granted, but you couldn't drop

an engine in a vehicle without expecting trouble somewhere
down the line.

It seemed like too much for coincidence, all things considered. Carnes clutched his Mini-14 tight enough to bleach
his knuckles white. He had the safety off, his finger on the
trigger, and the piece was set for automatic fire. His nerves
were strung out tighter than piano wire, and anyone who
tried to set him up would—

Wham!

He saw the second airboat blow, since they were headed
back toward the wreckage of the first airboat. Granted, Carnes only caught it from the corner of his eye, since he was
checking out the water, looking for survivors, enemies, but
he saw enough. There was a white-hot flash, then smoke,
and he saw bodies spilling overboard, the pilot tumbling
from his high seat, slumping over the controls. No dead-
man's switch on that rig, Carnes realized as the swamp
buggy reared, sped forward, closing on a hard collision
course with the disabled airboat thirty feet in front of it.

The impact split both hulls. The second buggy slammed
through a loping forward roll, to splash down with the rear
end of its giant fan aimed straight at Carnes, whipping up
a storm of wind and swamp spray before the engine gave
out.

He scanned the bayou for a target, desperate to do something. He was leaning forward like a pointer, checking out
the darkness, when a gunner on the fourth swamp buggy
started to fire, short bursts toward the nearest hummock.
Spotlights turned in that direction, probing for the target.

Carnes couldn't tell what he was shooting at, nor did he
care. The Mini-14 stuttered in his hands, a long burst, vent-
ing fury on the night, the bayou, anything available. It was
a stupid waste of bullets, though, and he caught himself
when he had burned up maybe half a magazine. Somebody
on the other boat was thinking, too, and they convinced the
shooter over there to hold his fire.

A couple of survivors from the airboat crash were thrashing in the water, calling out for help. Tough, Carnes thought. They still had work to do before he started playing doctor. They were barely twenty feet from shore, and Carnes could have hopped or swum that far on the worst day that he ever had.

On second thought, *this* was the worst day of his life, bar none.

HIS FRAG GRENADES were gone, well spent, and Bolan waited for some sign that he had been discovered by his adversaries on the last two boats. A couple of them wasted bullets, firing on the hummock to Bolan's left, but they recovered their composure in another moment, slacking off the random fire as they approached the tangled wreckage of their sister craft.

He watched and waited, counting down the doomsday numbers in his head.

The two remaining boats were eighty feet apart, then seventy, their pilots throttling back, while gunners on the flat decks stared in all directions, no one absolutely clear on what had happened to their comrades or where the strike had come from. Bolan counted off eleven men still high and dry, some peering into the water as if they expected floating mines or a torpedo hurtling out of nowhere.

Sixty feet between them, closing in to fifty now. He watched and waited, sighting down the Colt Commando's barrel, with no mark in particular. The wreckage of the tangled airboats lay between them, with a few men thrashing feebly in the water, calling out for help.

He couldn't get them all with thirty rounds, not sweeping them with automatic fire or switching over to the semiauto mode and plinking human targets one by one. With fifty feet or so between the boats, a perfect sweep on one would leave the other warned and ready for him, gunners sighting on his muzzle-flashes in the darkness, pinning him before he had a chance to cut and run.

For Bolan to have any hope at all, he had to rob them of mobility. Not trash the airboats, necessarily, but rob them of their guiding hands. It would require precision work, and it would bring him under fire, but Bolan knew he had to take the chance.

The airboat on his right was closer, twenty yards or so, instead of thirty-five. He lined up his sights on the pilot, thankful that the buggy's driver's seat was elevated to allow for greater visibility in swampy areas, where reeds and rushes often towered over six feet tall. A sidelong glance to fix the second pilot's rough location in his mind, and Bolan let his index finger curl around the Colt Commando's trigger, taking up the slack.

He sent a 3-round burst downrange, already pivoting to bring the second airboat's pilot under fire as number one pitched from the saddle, going over with a splash. Ten faces swiveled toward the source of gunfire, nine guns tracking on the sound and muzzle-flashes, but they couldn't stop him squeezing off a second burst. His target jerked, slipping from the driver's seat as if his bones had turned to sand.

There was a fair chance, Bolan realized, that one or more of the surviving gunmen would be trained to drive an airboat, but their hearts and minds were zeroed on one mission at the moment—peppering their faceless enemy with sustained gunfire.

He gulped a breath and ducked beneath the scummy surface of the water, pushing off with his feet as bullets plunked into the murk around him, flayed bark from the cypress overhead. He kept his eyes closed, felt his way along with one hand while the other clutched his carbine, praying it would still fire when he surfaced.

He counted as he swam, stayed down for all of ninety seconds, traveling perhaps a dozen yards underwater. When he surfaced, Bolan took care to avoid great sucking sounds or splashing that would certainly have given him away. He breathed in through his nostrils, kept his mouth closed— there was no point swallowing the muck if he could help it—and a quick swipe with his left hand cleared his eyes enough for him to aim.

The airboats were approximately where he left them when he'd gunned the pilots down and made his dive. One boat's engine had stalled out, and Bolan concentrated on the other, where a chunky figure wearing overalls had climbed into the driver's seat and started grappling with the controls.

He sighted on the would-be pilot's face and squeezed.

"CAN ANYBODY DRIVE this thing?"

It made him feel like an idiot that he couldn't drive the boat himself, but Carnes was desperate now, and anyone who laughed at him or even flashed a sideways look was going in the drink with half his head blown off.

"I can," a guy named Rudy replied.

"Do it, then!"

His other troops were firing off into the darkness, burning up their ammunition as if they had targets they could see. A glance showed Carnes that the second boat was dead and drifting, no one in the driver's seat, the men on deck unloading on the nearest hummock, blasting it with everything they had.

He shouted to them, telling them to hold their fire unless they had a solid mark, but none of them could hear him, not with the shooting going on. A couple of the men on his boat did stop firing, the last one knocking off after Carnes grabbed him by the collar of his sweaty T-shirt, jerking him around.

"Enough, goddammit!"

Seconds later, the survivors on the second airboat stopped their shooting, two or three reloading weapons, crouching on the deck as if it helped to get down on their knees.

The airboat lurched a trifle under Carnes's feet. He shot a warning glance at Rudy, was about to speak, when the fill-in pilot's head exploded, blood and brains sucked backward through the buggy's giant fan. His headless body balanced for a moment on the driver's seat, then toppled to the deck.

Gunfire erupted all around him then, his soldiers firing at a brand-new set of muzzle-flashes, but the enemy was also firing back at them. A bullet hummed past Carnes's face, while others found the hardman standing inches to his left and took him down.

Before he knew it, much less had a chance to think about it, Carnes was in the water, paddling like a dog and making for the nearest hummock, wondering if there were snakes or gators in the water underneath him, whether all the shooting would have driven them away.

He hoped so, but it didn't make much difference.

A cottonmouth was nothing compared to automatic-weapons fire.

Behind him, he heard people shouting, shooting, dying. Carnes hoped his men were scoring hits, but the survival impulse had him going, big time. It was more important to find cover at the moment than to stand his ground and be a hero, when he couldn't even see the men who tried to kill him.

He was almost to the hummock, paddling hard, when one of the airboats exploded. It was nothing like the first two, this one. Even with the swamp's reek in his nostrils, he could smell the gasoline that spilled out from a punctured fuel tank. All it needed was a spark—one muzzle-flash, a bullet glancing off the engine housing—and the whole damned thing went up in flames. He glanced back at the floating bonfire, saw men thrashing in the middle of the flames and swallowed hard to keep from puking as he swam.

He reached the hummock and dragged himself ashore on mossy ground that felt like thick sponge rubber, scrambling well back from the water's edge, until the ferns and saw grass covered him. He didn't try to find out where the enemy was firing from or how many people were involved. He didn't need a ton of bricks to fall on top of him before he got the message.

Carnes knew he was lucky just to be alive.

He meant to stay that way, not press his luck or look a gift horse in the mouth.

The Mini-14 had to be trashed by now, he told himself, but he would ditch it anyway when he was closer to the fishing camp. With the explosions and sinking boats, it would be easy to concoct a tale explaining his survival. He was thrown clear when the boats collided, lost his rifle in the drink. Hell, maybe he was knocked out cold, the water bringing him around when he was just about to drown. Why not?

One thing for sure—those crispy critters on the airboat weren't about to contradict him. He could tell the story his way, and let Doobie Arnold try to find out any different if he cared to try.

The main thing was to stay alive.

Still breathing heavily from the exertion of his midnight dunking, Dwight Carnes turned back toward camp and started plodding through the darkness, praying for the sounds of combat to subside.

THE REST OF IT was mopping up. One airboat was left in running order, with the motor stalled, and half a dozen gunmen were in the water, mostly wounded, each and every one of them more interested in personal survival than in victory.

Bolan could have let the swamp take care of it, or leave

them floundering until a backup team was fit to travel from their camp, but he had already made up his mind to appropriate the one remaining airboat for himself, if he could get the engine started. It would save him time, and that was of the essence now, but he didn't want any gunners taking pot shots at him while he was making his retreat.

He drew the Ka-bar fighting knife and waded out to reach the nearest soldier. This one had a belly wound, and he was fading fast. The Executioner moved on.

He found another adversary moving toward the nearest hummock in an awkward half walk, half crawl through the water, dragging what appeared to be a broken leg. The gunner heard him coming, even with his own harsh breathing and the splashing of his sluggish progress, and turned around and raised an Uzi subgun.

"Who's that?"

Instead of answering him, Bolan closed the gap between them with long strides and drove the Ka-bar underneath the hardman's rib cage, twisting, feeling hot blood spurt across his wrist. The wounded man slumped backward, going limp in death as Bolan slid the blade free of his flesh and rinsed it clean.

Two more gunners remained between him and the airboat, but he found that one of them was floating facedown in the stagnant water, kept from sinking by air pockets in his denim jacket. Bolan slit the fabric as he passed and watched the body vanish, trailing bubbles in its wake.

There was one left that he could see, and Bolan had to estimate that any gunners hiding in the dark should probably have opened up on him by now. Of course, their weapons could be lost or water fouled, but that was fine. The darkness and his war paint made a clear ID impossible, and if the hypothetical survivors posed no threat, he had no interest in pursuing them.

The final hardman had already reached the lone surviving airboat, and was climbing painfully aboard when Bolan came up on his blind side, reaching out to tangle fingers in his stringy hair and drag his head back, opening the throat below his mangy beard with one sweep of the Ka-bar's blade. The shooter started flopping like a grounded trout, hands coming up in a pathetic bid to close his throat wound, blowing crimson bubbles from the new smile underneath his chin. Seconds later he was dead.

It took a little coaxing for the airboat's flooded engine to revive, but Bolan managed, waiting for a steady beat before he tested the controls. A moment later, he was skimming through the darkness, following the spotlight's beam, with Spanish moss and drooping cypress branches whipping past on either side. The night air blowing through his wet fatigues was a relief. It dried the muck and perspiration on his face, swept Bolan's hair back, made him squint.

No problem.

By the time his adversaries got a search party together and began to comb the bayou, he would be long gone. It would be hours, maybe days, before they found the airboat he had borrowed, and it wouldn't tell them anything.

It had been close there for a while, but he was still alive, still pushing it. He couldn't call the mission an unqualified success, but any firefight Bolan walked away from was a victory of sorts.

His opposition would be more alert next time, and that was fine.

The Executioner wouldn't have had it any other way.

3

New Orleans has a certain air about it: jazz and jambalaya, Mardi Gras and misery. The architecture is ornate in certain neighborhoods, high-tech in others, barely passable in districts where the poor are prone to congregate. New Orleans has the French Quarter, two airports, an assembly plant for NASA and a U.S. Navy air station. It also has a squalid ghetto and illegal immigrants who slave in sweatshops, rampant graft, narcotics, prostitution and a thriving underworld. Some Crescent City natives call it the Big Easy, but survival isn't easy on the streets.

Bolan was familiar with New Orleans from previous campaigns. He liked the city, in a grudging kind of way, but didn't underestimate its darker side. New Orleans could sneak up behind a man and drag him down if he let down his guard.

At present, the Big Easy was caught up in the preliminary stages of a gang war. The majority of residents were unaware of the impending storm, but they would hear the gory details when it broke. No ordinary drive-by clash between the ghetto homeboys, this, but something more.

Something demanding the attention of the Executioner.

The old-line Mafia had ruled New Orleans and environs for a century, beginning in the 1880s, but a federal task force, paid informants in the ranks and passing time had undermined Sicilian dominance. The last great capo died in 1989, with various indictments pending, while a number of subordinates were sent away to state and federal penitentiaries on charges ranging from extortion and racketeering to first-degree murder. The Honored Society hung on in New Orleans, a shadow of its former self, but the control of vice, narcotics and associated rackets had been seized by other willing hands.

The biggest, strongest hands belonged to Durwood "Doobie" Arnold, leader of a homegrown redneck syndicate referred to in the media and law-enforcement memos as the Dixie Mafia. In days gone by, the hard core of the gang would have been labeled "white trash"—a mélange of rednecks, outlaw Cajuns and the like, who had traditionally tended moonshine stills, burned crosses for the Ku Klux Klan and brawled in honky-tonks throughout Louisiana since the Civil War. White lightning, racial terrorism and sporadic muscle work for the Sicilians used to be their stock-in-trade before cocaine became the rage and federal agents started making inroads into the Marcello Family. These days, with Doobie Arnold at the helm, the Dixie Mafia controlled the lion's share of drug traffic, commercial sex, hijacking and extortion, from Port Arthur to Mobile. The outfit paid its dues at the state capital, in Baton Rouge, and at the local level in the parishes that mattered, greasing and making sure that certain sheriffs and police chiefs looked the other way. Political corruption was an old, old story in Louisiana, as in many other states. It was a fact of life that Doobie Arnold's people went to jail from time to time, but they were treated well inside, and those who kept their mouths shut knew their families would be taken care of while they were away.

In short, it was business as usual, no real change except the cast of characters...until the Haitians came to town.

In truth, they had begun arriving some two hundred years before the Mafia, when French explorers brought along the captive Africans who had been "seasoned" in the West Indies. Before emancipation, there were thousands of them working on the great plantations, making their white owners wealthy, hiding native customs and religion underneath a thin veneer of Western "civilization." On the side, they practiced voodoo—an evolved form of their native tribal witchcraft from the Old World—and hung on until the tide of freedom turned their way. These days, with thousands fleeing poverty, political unrest or criminal indictments back in Port-au-Prince, their ranks were bolstered by a new breed of assertive Haitians—some of whom, predictably, had learned to live outside the law.

Jamaican mobsters called their gangs "posses," and while they had no real connection to the Haitian gangs, beyond an occasional common narcotics supplier, media reports had a tendency to pin the "posse" tag on Caribbean criminals across the board. If anything, the Haitians seemed more ruthless in their violence—no small admission, since Jamaican gangsters were well-known for their policy of shooting first and skipping questions altogether. It wasn't unusual for victims of the Haitian gangs to wind up being tortured, mutilated after death—if they were lucky—sometimes with the head and one or both arms missing from the crime scene. Scholars who attributed the grisly doings to pervasive faith in voodoo had initially been ridiculed by self-styled "experts" in the FBI, but that view had been drastically revised in recent months, with the arrest of Haitian narcodealers who erected voodoo altars in their homes, complete with sacrificial chickens, goats and jars of clotted blood.

Less interested in their religion than in the crime wave they had touched off in America, Mack Bolan had enough experience to know that faith could sometimes factor into motive, even make a superstitious criminal believe he was invincible. His own experience with homicidal cults along the Tex-Mex border and in America's heartland had prepared him to accept the fact that anything was possible.

What Bolan needed, at the moment, was a way inside.

And if his luck held out a little longer, it might be within his grasp.

"YOU LOOK LIKE SHIT," Doobie Arnold said, sipping at his first beer of the morning while he stared at Dwight Carnes.

"I been out in the swamp all night."

"At least you made it back. A couple dozen other boys wish they were standing in your place."

"I told you how that happened, Doobie."

"Yeah, you did. I'm wondering, should I believe you."

"Huh?"

The sweat was beading on Carnes's forehead now, despite the air-conditioning in Arnold's office. That was one way you could tell a man was lying, if he started to sweat like a farmhand when you asked him simple questions.

"I mean to say, you had some run of luck last night," the leader of the Dixie Mafia went on. "First thing, these bad-ass mothers miss you when they're shooting up the camp, then you go chasing them across the bayou, twenty guns to back you up, and you're the only one who makes it back."

"It happened like I told you," Carnes stated, sounding peevish now.

"I'm sure it did...up to a point." Another sip of beer kept Arnold's whistle wet. "The thing I'm havin' trouble with is how you got yourself knocked cold just when the action started gettin' hairy and them other boys went up in smoke, you know? I mean, we found some of them with their throats cut, Dwight. That takes time. It means the opposition got up close and personal, you get my drift."

"I don't see—"

"What I'm askin' is, if you were lyin' out there like a fuckin' mackerel, with your lights out, how's it come to be nobody cut *your* throat?"

Carnes had to ponder that one for a minute, screwing up his face like he was working on a long-division problem in his fifth-grade math class, right before he made his mind up that he'd had enough of higher education.

"I know what it must have been," he said at last.

"Do tell."

"When I came around, I'd washed up in between a couple of cypress boles. Seems like the fuckers must have missed me in the dark, while they were goin' for the buggy."

"Still, it's funny you're the only one they missed."

"I don't know what to tell you, Doobie."

"How about the truth, you lyin' sack of shit?"

The color drained from Carnes's face as if someone had pulled the plug and let his blood run out. He licked his lips, tongue darting like a lizard's, back and forth across dry lips.

"Well, now," he said at last, "it could be that I wasn't knocked out cold, the way I thought. You know, the more I think about it, I was kind of groggy there, but seems like I could move a little. Must have been I crawled back in the saw grass, there, before I passed out all the way. They absolutely would have missed me, then."

"It couldn't be that you took off and left your brothers in the shit, now, could it?"

"Hell, no! Doobie, you know me!"

"That's why I'm askin', Dwight."

"So, you're tellin' me you wish I'd gotten killed?"

"I'm tellin' you I wish you had told the truth first time I asked you."

"Doobie—"

Arnold pushed the button underneath his desk. Five seconds later, Dog Flaven and Snake Johnson were in the office, flanking Carnes's chair.

"You ever read about the Yakuza?" He smiled at that, a private joke. "Just kidding, Dwight. Anyway, that's what the Japanese call gangsters over there. They got all kinds of rules that wouldn't make no sense to us, but one of them I kind of like. You want to hear about it?''

"Uh…"

"When one of them fucks up, he has to tell the boss he's sorry, but he can't just say it, see? That ain't near good enough. No, what he does, he takes and cuts one of his fingers off and gives it to the boss, for an apology. Guy keeps on fuckin' up, he gets short-handed in a hurry, see?''

Carnes tried to smile. "That's pretty weird," he said.

"I like it, though. It shows respect." He raised his eyes to Flaven and Johnson. "Y'all take Dwight to the farm and teach him some respect. Cut somethin' off. I don't care what."

Carnes bolted from his chair, but his guards were faster, fists like hams colliding with his skull and dropping him before he had a chance to speak. They dragged him out and closed the door as Arnold finished off his beer and crumpled up the can, one-handed.

Carnes wouldn't be returning from the farm. It was a special kind of place, that fenced-in patch of bottom land outside Meraux, where Doobie cultivated alligators for the meat and hides. It was a way to launder money and dispose of nasty little problems, all at once.

Hell, even gators had to eat.

As for the rest of it, he had no reason to believe that Carnes could enlighten him about who had hit the fishing camp or why. The yellow son of a bitch had been too concerned with looking out for number one to get a line on who pulled off the raid. It would be Arnold's job, as usual, to scout around and beat the bushes, put his eyes and ears to work on finding out who was responsible.

But if he had to guess, he would have put the finger on the Haitians. Smart bastards had been looking for a way to cut themselves a slice of his pie since they had washed ashore, some of them crying for political asylum, others sneaking in and hiding from the immigration people just like any other wetbacks you could think of.

It was time to teach the whole damned bunch of them a lesson they wouldn't forget, and Doobie Arnold was the man to drive that lesson home. Of course, he needed proof to satisfy himself that his first instinct was correct, but that shouldn't be hard to come by.

Once he had it, Doobie Arnold told himself, the shit would *really* hit the fan.

TOM CARLISLE'S FATHER would have said he looked as if he had been ridden hard and put away wet. They actually used to talk that way in Oklahoma, and perhaps still did, for all he knew. It had been fifteen years since Carlisle found the time to visit home. Not that he had a reason to these days. The family was gone now, everybody dead or scattered to the four winds, with a brother in Chicago and another in L.A., his baby sister living in New York.

Could you call that living? Carlisle asked himself, and had to smile. Like he was doing so much better with the DEA. Big federal agent, right. He couldn't even stop his partner getting killed, when he was on the inside of the gang that did the dirty work.

They had forgiven him at headquarters, of course, kept telling him that it wasn't his fault. He knew the truth, knew what the rest of them were thinking—that Carlisle couldn't pull his weight and had let his partner down.

He wasn't the only brother in the agency, but there had been some eyebrows raised on this job, sending him to infiltrate the Haitian syndicate, while his partner—his white partner—came into the game as a buyer, the two of them working both ends against the middle to hit a grand slam.

Except it hadn't quite worked out that way. He didn't have the first clue as to how the posse blew Ferris Burke's cover. Carlisle hadn't been consulted, and they passed him over when they were selecting members of the hit team. It had come as a complete surprise, the call from his control advising him that Burke was dead—no, make that *butch-ered*—asking him if he could hold the fort alone or if he wanted out.

That would have been the capper, right. First black Tom lets his partner die, then weasels out of the assignment like the coward some of his white colleagues already believed he was.

He told the brass that he would stick it out, no matter what, and they had let him stew for several days before the callback, with a news flash that he had another contact coming in. Mike Belasko was the stranger's name, and they had fixed a date for Carlisle to connect with him in Kenner, up the coast from the Big Easy at a little diner out on Vintage Drive.

It had to be some kind of joke, Carlisle thought as he pulled into the diner's parking lot. The brothers they were used to seeing out this way came around the back door to deliver produce, maybe clean up in the kitchen. One good thing about it, though: if anybody from the posse tried to follow him out here, they would stand out like black beans on a bed of rice.

He parked the Lexus GS 300 nose-in toward the diner, smiling to himself as he imagined Sheriff Bubba wondering exactly what a black man did to get himself a forty-thousand-dollar ride. Bubba's first guess would be grand theft auto, but the registration papers in the glove compartment would have proved him wrong. The next guess would be drugs—it was the kind of vehicle that dealers had been turning to, of late, in place of the traditional Merce-des-Benz—and Bubba would have been exactly right.

Another bitter smile creased Carlisle's face. He thought about those books and movies from the fifties, all about the gallant G-men working undercover as they fought to save the world. He pictured his life story, flashed across the sil-ver screen: "I was a dealer for the DEA."

That kind of story wouldn't sell these days, when people were fed up with drugs, gangs, drive-bys and the other shit that went along with dealing. Any time you saw a black man in the movies these days, he was either Wesley Snipes or he was dealing crack.

The diner wasn't large, but it was nice enough. The air-conditioning was turned up high, to beat the steam heat simmering outside. The sign said Seat Yourself, and Carlisle did as he was told, taking a corner booth off to the left, where he could watch the kitchen and the front door simultaneously. He sat with his back against the wall.

They didn't teach you that in the academy. It came with working in the field and knowing every meal, each drink, could be your last. He wore the blue Armani blazer open, granting easy access to the automatic pistol holstered in a horizontal rig beneath his arm.

The waitress was a white gal in her early forties. She took one look at Carlisle and immediately copped an attitude, one eyebrow arched like she expected trouble, moving toward his booth with jerky little steps.

"Help you?"

"I'm meeting someone," Carlisle said. "I'll start with coffee and check the menu while I wait."

"One cup of coffee."

There were cups already on the table, but she came back with a laminated menu and a coffeepot, filling Carlisle's cup halfway.

"Think you can spare it?"

She was working on a retort, but it cost too much in terms of mental energy. Instead, she made a sour face and topped the coffee off. She was just about to turn and stalk away when Carlisle's contact breezed in through the swing doors.

No doubt. He had to be the man.

They had supplied him with the name but no description of the man he was supposed to meet. Carlisle assumed he would be white, the way their minds worked at the agency, but this was something else. The new arrival had a soldier's bearing and a killer's eyes. He graced the waitress with a smile and slid into the booth, across from Carlisle.

"Get you somethin'?" the waitress asked.

"Coffee's fine, for now."

"Yes, sir."

She put a little something extra in her walk as she was leaving, but Mack Bolan didn't seem to notice.

"Mr. Carlisle, I presume?"

"That's right. And you're Belasko."

"Right."

The Executioner put faith in his ability to judge men at a glance. This one was strong but troubled. No surprises there. He wondered if Tom Carlisle was a cowboy of the sort that DEA and ATF produced in such abundance these days, or if he would prove to be a solid soldier on the firing line. Losing a partner wasn't his fault necessarily, but it could tip him over the edge.

"We might as well get down to business," Bolan said.

"Suits me."

"I understand you've got a leg up with the local posse."

"I'm inside," Carlisle told him. "Nothing major yet, of course. They try you out on different things, see how you do. I've brought a couple shipments home the past few weeks. They're satisfied so far."

"What happened to your partner?" Bolan asked, cutting to the heart of it.

"They burned him," Carlisle said. "Don't ask me how. Nobody said a word to me. Hell, if they thought I was connected to him, *I'd* be dead, you know?"

"I understand they questioned him."

"That's not for sure. They cut him up, all right, no doubt about it, but that doesn't mean they were interrogating him, know what I'm saying?"

"Spell it out," Bolan said.

"Voodoo," Carlisle told him. "Can you spell that? Every move these crazy bastards make, they ask Damballah or some other bullshit spirit from the other side. It's like some kind of freak show, with the rum and chickens, throwing salt around and dancing with a snake, all kinds of shit like that."

"And human sacrifice?"

"They mostly do the goats and chickens, but every now and then they have some kind of special celebration, like a festival or something. Damballah needs a special offering, or maybe they just want to make a point, you know? Carve up a white man, leave him where you know the body will be found and people talk. It doesn't hurt to have the other side believing you'll do anything it takes. Same thing with the Colombians, when they cut someone's throat and pull his tongue out through the hole. It sends a message. If it fits in with their religion, hey, so much the better. If it wasn't for the rituals, they'd think of something else to get the point across."

"But they believe in what they're doing?" Bolan asked.

"The voodoo shit? I'd say. I've heard some of them say they were invisible or bulletproof. None of them were laughing when they said it."

Bolan heard the waitress coming back and forced a smile.

"Y'all ready?"

"Yes, indeed."

He ordered scrambled eggs and bacon, with a short stack on the side and some orange juice. Carlisle went for the gravy biscuits, with a side of sausage links. The waitress sashayed toward the kitchen on her four-inch heels, and Bolan reckoned they had fifteen minutes, give or take, before she came back with the food.

"Let's talk about the operation."

"Right." If Carlisle was surprised to leave the subject

of his partner's death, he didn't let it show. "What do you need?"

"Chapter and verse."

"Okay. The big man is Philippe Bouchet. He runs the posse, calls the shots. I get the feeling he's got someone calling *his* shots, back in Haiti, but he's definitely top dog with the voodoo brothers in New Orleans. Got a stone-cold killer named Louis Germaine who backs him up, like what the old guard used to call an underboss, you know?"

"I've heard the term," Bolan said.

"Anyway, I calculate they've got a hundred guys on payroll, give or take. It doesn't sound like much, compared to Doobie Arnold's outfit, but remember that a fairly high proportion of the black community down here—poor blacks, especially—still buy that voodoo rap. They won't come out and say it to your face—especially not *your* face, if you follow me—but there it is. You look around their houses and apartments, you'll find little charms or dolls, an altar here and there with candles on it, and a little dab of something looks like red nail polish, but it isn't. Okay?"

"I hear you."

"So, Philippe and Louis move some major weight. They bring it in on shrimp boats, sneak it through the bayous, maybe run an air drop every now and then. Same kind of shit the white boys pull. Now, Doobie Arnold wants to think he's got the game sewed up, but no white man controls what happens with the brothers after dark. Not the Marcello Family, not Sheriff Bubba, not the Klan—nobody. They can throw their weight around, all right, make people grin and shuffle, but they always go back home. And life goes on."

"Bouchet and Arnold have a rumble coming," Bolan said. He didn't phrase it as a question.

"You got that right, cousin. Doobie's made a couple moves against Philippe already, nothing big, but he could get his ticket punched if he doesn't watch himself."

"I'm counting on it," Bolan said.

"Say what?"

"I'm curious about your angle with the posse. You're obviously not a Haitian. Why should they trust you?"

Carlisle rubbed the fingers of one hand against his cheek and held them up for Bolan to inspect. "It doesn't rub off," he said. "I might not have the best blood, to their way of thinking, but I'm blood, you follow me?"

"That's it?"

"You had to be there, man."

"So, what's your cover?"

"I'm a local dealer, middleweight. They tell me I can join the posse and be rich, or find myself another playground. Simple."

"And they trust you?"

"To a point," Carlisle replied. "Like you said, I'm not a Haitian. It's equivalent to the Sicilian thing, I guess. You got your hard core, and your *hard* hard core. The rest are players, out there on the fringe. And then there's whitey."

"Well, it's good to know they're thinking of me."

"All the time, believe it. First, they want your money. Somewhere down the road, they'll want your soul."

The waitress brought their breakfasts, setting the plates in front of them. She kept her eyes on Bolan as she said, "Y'all think of anything you need, just give a whistle."

"Thanks," he said. "I'd say we're fine."

"So, what's the plan?" Carlisle asked after the woman retreated to the register.

"Eat breakfast," Bolan said.

"And after that?"

He looked up from his eggs and found Carlisle watching him.

"I don't know how much you were told," he said at last.

"The usual—not much."

"I'm not with DEA."

"I figured that."

"Let's say I handle jobs where prosecution isn't always feasible."

"Which means?"

"Exactly what you think it means," Bolan replied. "You've already given me a start. It would be helpful if you could supply me with a list of names, addresses, things like that, but if you'd rather not—"

"Hey, wait a second. Are you saying—?"

"That you're not obliged to help beyond this point, is what I'm saying."

"Help you start a war, that is."

"You've got the war already," Bolan said. "I'd like to see the good guys win."

4

Bolan's first target in the Crescent City was a crack house in suburban Terrytown, off Hector Avenue. The address was one of a dozen supplied by Tom Carlisle, written out in ballpoint on the flip side of a paper place mat from the diner. It would get him started, anyway, and he would find out where the campaign trail led him from there.

The neighborhood was mixed, low incomes the predominating factor in deciding who lived next to whom. A generation earlier, such mingling of poor whites and blacks in Dixie would have been unthinkable, a cause for brawling in the streets and crosses burning in the night. Some fighting still went on, of course—human nature wasn't changed with a list of rules and regulations—but the old-line residential color bars had long since been removed from local ordinances. Where they still survived, it was an economic issue for the most part, separating the haves from the have-nots.

The color that mattered most in New Orleans these days was currency green.

The Executioner motored past the crack house in his rented Buick Skylark, checking out the target as he passed. The place didn't appear to be a fortress, like some L.A. rock houses that needed tanks to breach the first line of defense, nor was it marked with gang graffiti as a signal to police and to the neighborhood at large. As Bolan passed by, doing twenty miles per hour, he could see an effigy of some kind on the front door of the house, dead center. It was manlike in appearance, maybe burlap, stuffed with rags or straw, whatever. Bolan couldn't see the face, if it had one, but two long feathers dangled from the figure's stubby legs—one white, one black. The effigy was held in place by something that resembled a slender metal spike or knitting needle, driven through its chest into the door.

A voodoo warning? Did it keep the other predators at bay?

He drove around the block, parked in the shadow of a vacant building that had once been a convenience store and locked the car. He primed the tamperproof alarm and hoped that it would be enough. The neighborhood didn't intimidate him, in itself, but Bolan did not like the thought of being left on foot, however briefly, when he had important work to do.

It was a risk to make the strike in daylight, but he hadn't felt like sitting through another day inactive, waiting for the sun to set. No one appeared to watch him as he parked the Buick, and his outfit—denim jacket and a sport shirt over faded jeans and running shoes—would be a fair match for the garb of other white men in the neighborhood. His grooming was a weak spot—Bolan could have let his hair grow for a week or two and skipped a few shampoos—but no one sober was about to challenge him once they had glimpsed his eyes. As for the drinkers, they should be in bed or sweating out hangovers on the job instead of wandering around the streets of Terrytown.

He walked back to the crack house, pausing long enough to double-check the mini-Uzi slung beneath his jacket on a leather swivel rig. He also carried the Beretta 93-R, unscathed by its dunking in the bayou, in an armpit holster on the other side. The hardware made his jacket seem a little bulky—and it was already out of place, in the Louisiana summer—but concealment won the day. He passed a few pedestrians along his walk back to the target, but none of them spared the stranger a second glance.

They were all strangers here.

The curtains were closed on all sides of the crack house, but that didn't mean he wasn't being watched. They could have peepholes, periscopes, somebody peering through a crack between the curtains, maybe even spotters in the house or yard next door. He scaled the fence and touched down on the dry brown grass inside.

It was a short jog to the house, and Bolan expected an alarm to go at any time. When he reached the back door unopposed, he had to figure those inside the house were high, asleep or too complacent with their magic shield in place to mount a proper guard.

There was another burlap doll pinned to the back door of the crack house. Bolan tugged it loose and stuffed it in a pocket, stooping while he pressed a thumb-sized plastic charge against the doorjamb, near the lock, and put ten seconds on the timer. Stepping back, he crouched and cupped his hands to his ears, waiting for the door to blow.

He was in motion well before the shock waves of the blast subsided, shouldering aside the ruined door and going in behind his Uzi through a haze of dust and smoke. The back door opened on a combination dining room and kitchen, and two black gunmen were seated at a folding table, playing cards. They lurched erect as Bolan entered, reaching for their guns, but the Uzi chopped them to pieces with a sweeping burst that left them stretched out on the floor.

The Executioner kept on moving, following the sound of voices, through a hallway leading to a pair of bedrooms where the intervening wall had been knocked down, creating lab space that was twenty feet by twelve. Three workers stood and gaped at Bolan, taken by surprise while they were cooking rock cocaine, their wide eyes almost comical above the surgical masks they wore. A fourth man in the room already had his pistol out and blasting, his bullets flying high and wide as he put speed above precision.

Bolan taught the shooter his mistake, a short burst from the Uzi opening his chest and slamming him against the nearest wall. The workers tried to scatter, but they had already lost the chance. He shot them on the run, a few rounds each to drop them in their tracks, not really caring whether they were dead or wounded at the moment.

Bolan checked out the remainder of the house and found himself alone. How long before one of the neighbors called police? If he was lucky, it could be a while, and longer yet before a squad car rolled in to answer the call. In some parts of L.A. and New York, he knew, the law-abiding locals wouldn't even phone it in if dealers shot each other. It was pest control, and no one really cared, as long as a stray round didn't kill some decent person down the street.

Before he left, he took a couple of incendiaries from his pocket, twisted off their caps to start them cooking, then deposited the fire sticks with a stash of bottled ether in the lab. In sixty seconds, there would be enough heat in the crack house for Philippe Bouchet to feel it in his office on the other side of town.

A handful of civilians stood and watched Bolan leave the crack house. As Bolan scaled the fence, retracing his approach, he heard somebody whistle, and a few of the spectators started clapping, giving him a weak round of applause.

Round one had been a clean sweep for the Executioner, but he was barely getting started in New Orleans. He wasn't concerned about a voodoo curse, but there were men out there with guns, both black and white, who wouldn't hesitate to cut him down if they got half a chance.

His only safety lay in speed, audacity and nerve.

The Executioner was blitzing on.

FRANÇOIS EDMONDS WAS feeling no pain. He liked to toke the special reefer they imported from Jamaica—prime ganja from their Rasta brothers—anytime he had the chance.

And that was nearly all the time.

It wasn't like he needed it, of course. He liked it. Maybe even loved it, if he had to sit right down and quantify emotions. But he didn't let the reefer rule his life.

No way.

When he was working, for example, Edmonds took only a few quick hits to make him fit for duty, looking sharp and thinking sharp. Like now. It wasn't what you'd call a heavy job, standing watch outside a riverfront warehouse south of Tchoupitoulas Street, but it gave him something to do, looking busy, without having to break a real sweat.

The locals liked to bitch and moan about how hot it was this time of year, but they had never been to Haiti in the summertime, smelled garbage rotting in the streets, where dogs and human beings squatted side by side to defecate. The houses in Edmonds's old neighborhood, in Port-au-Prince, were made from sheets of corrugated tin and plywood. Air-conditioning was something from a science-fiction story, found in certain office buildings and the homes of "better" families. No matter how often Americans came back to help with guns and tanks, it seemed that nothing ever changed except the faces at the top.

Until he found his calling.

There was simple justice and a sense of satisfaction in the way he earned his living. Selling sweet dreams to the white man made him rich—by Haitian standards, anyhow—and it was all the sweeter, knowing that the dreams he sold had poison in them, slowly killing off the host.

Edmonds would rather sell than snort the hard stuff. Oh, he used it on occasion, to be sociable, but for the most part, ganja did him right. Cocaine was for the ones whose world had suddenly outgrown their dreams, and for the ones whose dreams were stillborn in the dust.

François Edmonds had dreams of going back to Haiti in another year or two to start up his own exporting business. He wouldn't go into competition with Philippe Bouchet, of course; that would be crazy. But he might consult Bouchet, pick up a franchise, as it were, where he could deal with business of his own, instead of watching someone else's merchandise go by.

Right now, though, all he had to do was pull the warehouse watchdog gig, and it was getting old. He shifted in the warm shade, adjusting the chamois holster he wore over bare skin, beneath his baggy shirt, and wished he had some reefer now to help him chill. A toke or two would do it. Maybe he should duck inside and ask Marcel if he—

The blast was powerful enough to knock Edmonds completely off his feet. He tasted asphalt, scrambled up on hands and knees, one hand inside his shirt and groping for the big Glock 21 before he knew exactly what was happening. He shook his head to clear it, straightened to a kneeling posture and turned back to scope out the warehouse, a reek of something similar to cordite heavy in his sinuses.

The near wall of the warehouse had a bulge twelve to fifteen feet across and maybe eight feet high. It instantly reminded Edmonds of a giant blister, or perhaps a dent produced by heavy impact from inside.

He drew his pistol, knowing that he had to do something, even if he had no clear idea of what was happening. Bouchet stored drugs inside the warehouse now and then—Edmonds knew that much, but he had seen nothing in the way of lab equipment, arms or ammunition that would touch off an explosion.

He ran in the direction of the loading dock, his quickest access to the warehouse proper in the case of an emergency. Edmonds could smell the smoke before he got there, bringing water to his eyes. Still, his vision was clear enough for him to distinguish the white man standing on the loading dock, an Uzi submachine gun braced against his hip and pointed right at Edmonds's face.

"It's a done deal," the white man said. "Make it easy on yourself."

But what could he have told Philippe Bouchet, the man who took him out of Port-au-Prince and paid him handsomely for very little work? More to the point, how could his willing failure be explained to Baron Samedi or Damballah?

There was no way he could pull it off; that much was guaranteed. The Uzi had him covered, while his own Glock pointed at the pavement underneath his feet. The white man merely had to twitch his finger at the first sign of a hostile movement from Edmonds, and he was dead. Unless...

It was time to test the power of Damballah, see if he was really bulletproof.

Strike three.

CARLISLE TOLD HIMSELF that what he was doing, basically, was following his orders from the brass at DEA. They told him to cooperate by any means appropriate with Mike Belasko, and they left it up to him to decide what the definition of "appropriate" should be. It was their way of sticking Carlisle with the booby prize, if anything went wrong.

Belasko had to have some kind of sanction from upstairs to pull the kind of moves he had in mind. It was an undercover agent's wet dream, rolling out on the offensive for a change and kicking ass instead of standing by and playing yes-man for some low-life piece of shit who shouldn't be allowed to live, much less get rich on someone else's misery, then tie the courts up for a decade with his frivolous appeals.

There was a part of Belasko's plan that got to Tom Carlisle where he lived, but then again, it made him nervous, too. A black man in America knew what could happen when the vigilantes started riding. Even on those rare occasions when they started with the best intentions, only taking out the hard-core human garbage, there inevitably came a point when the incentive to continue punishing the bad guys outweighed any public good. From hunting hard-ass criminals who openly defied the law, the vigilantes branched out into public morals, weeding out free thought and watching out for anyone so different from the herd that he or she appeared to threaten law and order by the mere act of existing. Jews were good when it came down to picking scapegoats, but you couldn't always spot them, once they were a few blocks from the synagogue. Blacks, now, that was a different story. You could spot them all day long and use the FBI's raw crime statistics to support whatever claims you chose to make about the prevalence of crime in black communities.

Carlisle understood that Mike Belasko would be hunting whites—the idiots from Doobie Arnold's mob—as well as Haitian dealers, but he still felt strange participating in the kind of action that would normally send people off to federal prison rather than placing letters of commendation in their files.

It felt like he was selling out his people and himself.

But Philippe Bouchet and company were most emphatically *not* Tom Carlisle's people. Nationality aside, they were drug dealers, smugglers, murderers, fanatic voodoo cultists. If you closed your eyes to color, Carlisle had no more in common with the posse than he did with any neo-Nazi skinhead on the street. He didn't buy the argument that black men had to stick together, right or wrong, that any charge filed on a black defendant by the "white man's law" was automatically a frame-up by the racist pigs. Carlisle had seen too much while working with the DEA to put much faith in fellow men of *any* color.

There was right, and there was wrong.

But where did Belasko's private war fit in the universal scheme of things?

One reason Carlisle played along was to assuage his sense of guilt. A piece of him had died with Ferris Burke, his murdered partner, slashed to ribbons by the very animals Belasko would be hunting in the next few hours. And if the stranger managed to upset Doobie Arnold's little business while he was at it, what was wrong with that?

White scum, black scum, the quickest way to get rid of it was to flush it down the drain.

Such notions would have shocked Carlisle when he graduated from the DEA academy. He was supposed to be a front-line soldier in the war on drugs, but there were so damned many rules he had to follow, paperwork to type up that the war on drugs became a big joke on America. If Ross Perot ever went looking for that great big sucking sound he used to talk about when he was running for the White House, Carlisle could have told him where to find it. Stand and watch the millions upon millions of tax dollars thrown away on interdiction programs that were doomed to fail because too many local cops—and some Feds, too—were getting paid by both sides to subvert the effort; doomed because the scumbag pushers had more civil rights than any of their victims or the officers who took them off the street; doomed from the start because the very politicians and celebrities who called for law and order in their ritzy neighborhoods were also snorting up and chilling out with the same poison they professed to hate like sin itself.

What kind of system was it when your public servants in the legislature automatically exempted themselves from every law they passed, then turned around and gave themselves another pay raise for a job well done? What kind of justice was it when the trials could be postponed for years on end with bullshit motions that would make a law-school freshman laugh his ass off? Where was law and order when white lawyers in New York filed suit to cancel random locker searches in the violence-ridden high schools of Detroit, whose civil liberties were they protecting by allowing more guns into classrooms that had already become a battleground?

Carlisle would help Belasko—for a while, at least—because the man seemed to have an angle on the action in New Orleans. Playing Arnold and Bouchet against each other, helping out with some strategic punches of his own...it just might work. And DEA agent was free to bail out at any time; the two of them were crystal clear on that, up front.

He owed that much to Ferris, paying back the bastards who had turned his partner into so much butchered meat. It could be him, tomorrow, just as easily.

Unless he got them first.

He would keep a sharp eye on Belasko, feed him information from the streets and see where he was going with his one-man war. If it began to veer off track, Carlisle could always cut him loose. But if he played it straight, stayed focused on his mission and kept slugging...hell, it might be worth a shot to try to join him on the firing line.

Not yet, though.

Carlisle was daydreaming, and dreams could get you killed if you mistook them for reality. He had to walk a fine line as it was, between Belasko and Philippe Bouchet. They had a cutout number set, where they could get in touch with one another on an hour's maximum delay, but that would do nothing for Carlisle if he dropped the ball and someone put a pistol to his head.

A person did his best, he told himself, and anything beyond that was gravy.

Right.

But gravy didn't taste so fine if you were in the cooking pot yourself.

SHARE AND SHARE ALIKE, Bolan thought as he parked his Skylark in a lot off Royal Street, on the northern edge of the French Quarter. He was going after Doobie Arnold's people this time, giving his Haitian enemies a little breathing room, some time to stop and wonder who was ragging them the past few hours.

He was reasonably confident that they would make the right decision in the end.

He walked southeast on Madison, to Chartres, turned northeast from there and paced off half a block before he found the address he was seeking. The apartment building was old and might have passed for quaint, except that Bolan knew the owner of the building and his tenants.

Doobie Arnold held the deed, through intermediaries, and he rented all the flats to trusted underlings. The red-brick structure was a barracks, in effect, with twenty-five or thirty gunners living on the premises at any given time.

Tough odds, but Bolan felt like he was on a roll.

It had begun to drizzle, so Bolan had a reason for the lightweight plastic slicker covering the Colt Commando slung beneath his right arm and the Beretta 93-R worn beneath his left. No one gave him a second glance as he stood, checking out the old apartment building, then made his way inside.

The lobby was a Spartan cubicle, no furniture of any kind, no decorator touches anywhere, unless you counted rows of rusty-looking mailboxes that had been set into one wall immediately on the left as he walked in. The place smelled musty, sweat and mildew mingling to create a rank odor. Bolan glanced down at the carpet, wondering if it was brown when it had been installed.

The lobby elevator dated back to Prohibition days, and Bolan took the stairs. There was a chance they could have sentries on the landings, but it was easier to watch an elevator come and go. Besides, the Dixie Mafia had ruled the roost around New Orleans for the best part of three years. The previous night's adventure on the bayou notwithstanding, it was doubtful any of the urban troops would be expecting an attack on their sleeping quarters.

Bolan started up the stairs, the Colt Commando out and cocked. There was no point in hiding it anymore, when every tenant of the building was an enemy. There could be girlfriends on the premises, something like that, but they would have to take their chances with the big boys. Bolan wouldn't fire on noncombatants, given any kind of choice at all, but if they took up arms to help the home team, everyone was fair game.

His plan was relatively simple: hike up to the top floor and begin his sweep from there, kill anyone he saw as he was marching back down to the street. It put him in a corner, with a block of hostile guns between himself and daylight, but the tactic also had advantages. Once he was in the game, his full attention would be focused on the lobby and its exit, five floors down. Whatever stood between him and the street became an obstacle, and Bolan was an expert at removing obstacles. Surprise would help him—anyone alert to the potential danger of attack would clearly be expecting trouble to approach them from the street—and if he worked it right, a touch of chaos in the ranks could put survivors in a rush to get downstairs, thus giving him more cover and a nice diversion.

He reached the fifth floor unobserved and unopposed, no hardmen stirring from their rooms, though several had their doors propped open, spilling country music into the corridors. He kept each hallway covered with the automatic carbine as he passed, then hurried up the next two flights of stairs, prepared for anything, until he reached the top.

From that point on, it would be butcher's work.

The point of his incursion was to take a fighting unit from the Dixie Mafia and turn it into dog meat. He hadn't come to intimidate, interrogate or simply terrorize. He had no message to impart, no ultimatum to deliver.

He was there to kill, and there was no time like the present to begin.

He drew the 93-R with its custom sound suppressor attached, and held the pistol in his left hand, cocked and ready, while the automatic rifle balanced in his right, the butt wedged tight between his elbow and his ribs. If possible, he would prefer to get a few points on the scoreboard without rousing every shooter in the house, but he would play the cards as they were dealt.

To that end, Bolan passed the first two sets of facing doors, all closed, and moved on to the last pair at the far end of the hall. One door was open all the way, on his left. Across the hall, the other door was cracked, a wedge of pale light showing, nothing to suggest a lurker on the other side.

He stepped into the open doorway, the Beretta leading, while his rifle pointed back across the hall. He found a pair of unkempt denim boys relaxing on a swaybacked couch and watching urban cowboys line dance on the Nashville Network. Bolan could have interrupted them, to let them know Death had come calling, but he didn't see the point. Instead, he punched a silenced parabellum mangler through each skull and watched them slump together, lifeless eyes still locked on the TV.

He crossed the narrow hallway, toed the second door aside and peered into the squalid room. Nobody home, and he could only wonder if the tenant had been watching television with his bud across the hall.

If they were living one man to a room in here, he had a maximum of thirty guns to deal with on his way back to the street, not counting drop-ins who might come around to shoot the breeze and drink a beer or six.

The next door coming up, on Bolan's left, was locked. He let it go and crossed the hall. This time, the knob turned at his touch, and Bolan inched the door back, peering through into a rundown parlor as the portal widened.

Movement at the corner of his vision halted the Executioner, made him blink as Sasquatch walked into the living room. A second glance corrected the impression and confirmed his adversary was a human male, albeit one whose birthday suit resembled a gorilla costume, right down to the sagging paunch and dangling arms. There might be muscles underneath that mass of tangled body hair, but Bolan had no interest in the guy's physique. Right now he was unarmed, and that was all that mattered.

Bolan shouldered through the doorway, sighting down the slide of his Beretta into Bigfoot's startled face. The guy recovered swiftly, though, and started shouting for his buddies, raising hell, as if he understood it was the only option open to him.

The Executioner shot him where he stood, but it was already too late. Emerging from the room, he saw two doors spring open between him and the staircase, shooters coming to find out which one of their associates was making all the noise.

He could have dropped them both with the Beretta, but the shouts of his last victim had already echoed through the house, and one of those responding triggered two rounds from a .38 before the Executioner could act. He swept them with a burst from the Commando, dropping both men in their tracks.

And that was all she wrote for stealth.

No one emerged from the remaining rooms, and Bolan gave up waiting for them, moving toward the stairs. From somewhere below, a babble of excited, worried voices rose to Bolan's ears, men shouting questions, cursing, calling for a volunteer to go upstairs to find out what was happening.

Bolan armed a frag grenade and dropped it down the stairwell, leaning well across the banister, then jumping back as time ran out. Somebody growled a warning, but it came too late. The blast sent shock waves through the floor, and a mushroom cloud of smoke and dust ascended through the stairwell, nearly gagging him.

He took a firm grip on the Colt and started down the stairs.

5

The Silver Chalice magic shop was located on Jackson Street, midway between the Mississippi River and New Orleans General Hospital. It opened on the stroke of 9:00 a.m., six days a week, and its proprietor had been late only twice in seven years.

Marianne Lacroix was thirty-four years old, but she possessed an ancient soul. That fact had been confirmed by tarot readings, several palmists and a three-month foray into past-life regression hypnosis, all supporting what she had, in truth, known for herself since she was nine or ten years old.

She knew that she had lived before, not once, but many times.

And she would live again.

That kind of knowledge put life in radical perspective, alien to ninety-five percent of those who passed her on the streets each day. They all had other lives behind them, too, but never knew it. Their ignorance prevented them from working off accumulated karmic debts in timely fashion and retarded evolution toward the end goal of Becoming, but she understood that every man and woman had to proceed through life in his or her own way.

Each morning, rain or shine, the heady smell of herbs was there to greet her when she opened up the shop. She stocked more than 250 herbs in all, selected for their special properties, for use in magic rituals, in amulets or mojo bags.

Agrimony protected users while they slept. Bayberry brought prosperity. Hawthorne enhanced fertility and happiness. Lemon verbena opened up the soul to love. Poke bolstered courage, and could sometimes break a hex. Slippery elm stopped spiteful gossip. Tonka beans could make the fondest wish come true...or maybe not.

Besides the herbs, she carried charms and amulets, gemstones and magic candles, books and magazines on the occult, lapel pins, bumper stickers and a full range of ritual items for magic practitioners, white, black and gray. She believed in them all, had long since made her choice, but free will was the law of the universe. It wasn't her place to say which gods deserved respect, and which should be ignored. The so-called Christian Right judged others every day, without her help, and they would doubtless view her as a candidate for everlasting hellfire if they even knew she was alive.

No, it wasn't her place to judge.

And that was why the late-night call from Amos Carr had so disturbed her, almost prompting her to break her private rule and close the shop today. It wouldn't work, of course.

Avoiding the inevitable was a futile exercise for sterile minds.

A man was coming to ask questions. Carr said he was a good man, but the term was open to interpretation. Lacroix had checked the cards the previous night, as soon as she got off the telephone, and what she saw had been disturbing. Strength and Justice figured prominently, and the Lovers made a brief appearance, but the Devil lurked nearby, and Death was omnipresent, riding its pale horse across a field of bones.

Not her death, necessarily—she hadn't cared to make the forecast personal, in that respect—but it was coming. There were people in New Orleans, blithely taking care of business even now, who wouldn't live to see another sunrise.

Lacroix could feel a measure of their pain and sadness if she tried, but she deliberately kept that door shut tight.

She moved around the shop and tidied up, distracted by her apprehension. Amos Carr was a cop—*ex*-cop, she corrected herself—who spent his retirement investigating allegations of occult involvement in various crimes, advising law-enforcement agencies around the country and around the world on what to look for in apparent cult-related cases. He had cultivated friends among white witches, sorcerers, *santeros* and the like. When Lacroix last saw him, he was passing through New Orleans on the trail of a transient Christian cult that lured disaffected teens away from their affluent, dysfunctional families, promising a ticket to paradise in return for all their worldly goods. A few months later, she had read in the *Times-Picayune* about the cult leader's indictment on a list of state and federal charges that made the New Orleans Yellow Pages resemble a haiku by comparison.

She trusted Amos Carr, liked the open-mindedness that relegated his police mentality to a subordinate position when he talked about the Art. Of course, she realized he was a total cynic, no belief in anything beyond the here and now, but he wanted to understand the believers, follow their collective thought processes, even as he told himself they were a bunch of kooks.

She had agreed to speak with Mike Belasko as a favor to a friend. Carr didn't tell her what the man was doing in New Orleans, why he needed her—all that would come in time. For now, it was enough to know that he was dangerous and that he needed help.

It was her weakness, helping others. She sometimes used magic, when a friendly ear or helping hand wasn't enough, but it could lead to trouble.

Once upon a time, it almost got her killed.

She didn't know when Belasko would arrive or what he looked like. It would take care of itself, if she was meant to help him. Lacroix knew it was pointless to resist the Fates.

Still, she could put him off if what he asked of her was too outrageous. Marianne Lacroix was no one's puppet. If she helped this stranger, it would be on her terms, nothing forced about it, nothing that would interrupt her progress toward a higher plane of consciousness.

And she wouldn't expose herself to evil for the sake of showing off, testing herself. That lesson had been learned, and she didn't need a refresher course.

The front door opened, jangling a small brass bell. She turned from straightening a rack of magazines to find a tall, dark stranger watching her. His aura mingled kindness with a world of hurt. He might have been a healer, but his eyes told Lacroix he went the other way. He was a hunter and a warrior. Watching him, she felt her apprehension mount. She looked at him, but saw an image from the tarot.

Death.

THE SMELL OF HERBS and incense in the shop was almost overpowering, but Bolan breathed it in, willing his senses to adjust. The main thing was perception, visual and aural, checking out the woman and assessing what she had to say.

His contact was a thirty-something beauty, five foot six or seven, wearing a loose caftan with little or nothing underneath. The spirit of freedom was mirrored in her amber eyes. The lady's skin was the lightest possible café au lait, her straight brown hair fashioned into a stylish chignon.

"May I help you?" she asked.

"I'm Mike Belasko."

"Marianne Lacroix." She kept the handshake to herself.

"I got your name from Amos Carr," he said.

"I know. He called last night." She paused, then added, "He tells me you're a good man."

"That's debatable."

"He likes you, anyway," she said.

"It's mutual."

"You have some questions?"

"If you have the time."

She glanced around the shop and smiled. "I'm not exactly overrun with customers right now."

"Okay. I need to learn about voodoo."

"Check out *The Serpent and the Rainbow*. Davis knows his subject, even if he is a white man."

Bolan frowned. "I'd like to, but the problem is I'm on a deadline. I can't spare that kind of time."

"What brings you to New Orleans?"

The soldier answered with a question of his own. "Did Amos tell you how we met?"

"He said you worked together once."

"Well, there you go."

"That doesn't tell me anything. He mostly works with law enforcement. You don't look much like a cop."

"You're right. I'm not."

"Well, then?"

"I handle problems when the cops get stuck. You might call me a troubleshooter."

"And today, you're shooting trouble in New Orleans."

"That's about the size of it," he said. "I need some help."

The woman's evident reluctance didn't put him off. It was a safe and sane reaction in the circumstances. He wouldn't blame her if she turned him down.

"What kind of help?" she asked at last.

"Just information."

"Just?" She smiled at him, the way she might have at a child. "Knowledge is power, Mike. You know that, or you wouldn't be here. Please don't take me for a fool."

"I don't."

"All right, let's try again. What kind of information are you looking for?"

"The basics, for a start," he said. "Beyond that, anything you know about the link between voodoo and organized crime, whatever weak points a practitioner may have.''

"That's all?'' Her voice contained a note of sarcasm. "You're not out looking for the secret of the universe?''

"Some other time.''

"I could go on for hours, days,'' she said.

"Just let me have an abbreviated version.''

"All right, then. Would you like some herbal tea?''

"Sounds good.''

It was.

"Calm comfort,'' Lacroix informed him as she handed him the fragrant mug and sat down facing him, across a showcase filled with necklaces and amulets. "It helps relax the mind and nerves.''

"As long as I don't fall asleep while we're talking.''

"Not to worry.''

"So, voodoo,'' he prompted her.

"It comes from the Yoruba tribe's juju religion,'' she explained. "When they were shipped to the Caribbean as slaves, and on from there to the United States, they brought their gods and demons with them. To escape the white man's punishment for being 'heathens,' some worshipers disguised those gods with names they borrowed from the Christian saints, while others shunned such compromise, determined not to yield. They were compelled to pray in secret, fearing punishment—or even death—if they were caught. The faith was passed down to their children and their children's children, changing over time. Its variations all have different names today—voodoo among the Haitians and some black Americans, *candomble* or *macumba* in Brazil, *obeah* in Jamaica, *santeria* where Hispanics mix it with Catholicism. No two sects are quite the same, but they have common roots and share some basic rituals. You follow me?''

"So far,'' the Executioner replied.

"Voodoo acknowledges a pantheon of gods or spirits,

called *loas*," she said. "Damballah is the strongest, represented by a serpent. His right-hand man is Baron Samedi, lord of cemeteries and the dead, most often represented by an effigy consisting of a wooden cross, and dressed in a top hat and an old frock coat. His private cult of worshipers are called *bizango*. Back in Haiti, Papa Doc Duvalier encouraged superstitious peasants to believe that he was the physical incarnation of Baron Samedi. That belief did as much as the Tonton Macoutes to help his family rule for thirty years. Questions?"

"Not yet."

"Okay. Each voodoo cult is headed by a priest, the *houngan*, or a priestess, called a *mambo*. Male or female makes no difference in their power. It's experience and their connection to the spirit world that count. They influence Damballah and the other gods by means of offerings and sacrifice, anything from rum and money to the blood of goats and chickens. Sacrifice, as you may be aware, releases psychic energy and helps to open up communication with the gods."

"What about human sacrifice?" he asked.

It was the woman's turn to frown. "I've heard the stories, nothing I could swear to. Theoretically a human being could be sent as an ambassador to speak directly with the gods. His soul is captured by the priest or priestess who performs the sacrifice. He has no choice but to obey their orders in the spirit world. A measure of the *houngan*'s power clings to the ambassador, although the sacrificial victim cannot wield it by himself."

"So, what's the voodoo take on dealing drugs?"

"Aside from Satanism, which deliberately and systematically attempts to counter Christianity, occult religions don't waste time debating 'sin.' An act is evil if it violates the basic laws of nature or the universe, whatever. Some religions have a god who punishes such crimes, while others trust in nature to maintain a balance, yin and yang.

Disease may spring from conscious desecration of the body temple. Men who savage the environment destroy themselves as a result. Within that framework of belief, white and black magic are simply a matter of perspective. If you defend yourself with magic from an enemy's attack, that's white magic from your viewpoint. It's black, or evil, to the one on the receiving end. Drug dealers may run up a karmic debt from poisoning their customers, but voodoo—and especially its darker side, *quimbanda*—blesses any faithful supplicant.''

"That's a convenient faith," Bolan commented.

"No more so than Christianity," she said. "'For every one that asketh receiveth, and he that seeketh findeth, and to him that knocketh it shall be opened.' How many Christians out there pray for money or a new car every day?''

"I see your point. Are you familiar with the name Philippe Bouchet?''

A shadow seemed to pass across her face before she said, "I am, by reputation.''

"As a *houngan?*''

"As a murderer, devoid of conscience. There are rumors that he serves Damballah. Some say it's the other way around. In any case, he's not one of my customers.''

"I need to find his weakness," Bolan said.

"Offhand, I'd guess that would be greed, with ego running close behind. I emphasize the 'guess.' We've never met, you understand. I'd have a better chance of psycho-analyzing you.''

"A waste of time. Can you tell me how to hit him where he lives?''

"Would that be speaking metaphorically, or...?''

"What I have in mind is psy-ops," Bolan told her. "Call it head games with an application to the street.''

"I see.''

"As far as the specifics go, the less you know, the better off you'll be.''

"In that case," she replied, after a moment's hesitation, "there are several things I might suggest."

WHEN HE WAS GONE, she put the Gone to Lunch sign in her window, locked the door and stepped into the back room of her shop. Part of the ten-by-twenty room was storage space for merchandise. A cluttered desk and filing cabinets occupied one corner. Six square feet had been devoted to an altar. Nothing fancy: bare wood, braced on cinder blocks, with candles and the other necessary items carefully arranged.

As Lacroix was putting on her skull-bead necklace for protection and selecting special herbs for the same purpose, she reviewed brief snatches of her conversation with Mike Belasko.

Amos tells me you're a good man.

That's debatable.

An honest man, at least.

And from the little he had told her, and the insight she had gained from watching him, absorbing what he said and listening between the lines, Lacroix knew that Belasko was a man of violence. But she didn't sense that he was evil. There were times, she realized, when violent action was the only means by which aggression could be halted. Her beliefs placed a priority on prayer, negotiation, fellowship, but there were times when compromise accommodated evil and ensured a victory for psychic predators.

At such times, Lacroix believed, resistance was a sacred obligation, though its form might vary radically from one soul to the next. One might be moved to pray for guidance, while another took up arms against the common enemy. There was no contradiction in the two responses, merely recognition of their differences in temperament and physical ability.

She knelt and lit two candles mounted on the altar: white, for centering; black, for protection. Next, she placed a pinch of ginger in the small ceramic bowl before her, following with rosemary and thyme. The ginger was an herb of Mars, the ancient god of war, supposed to bring success and power. Rosemary was used for exorcism. Thyme was linked to Venus, bringing purity and psychic healing to the recipe. She crushed and stirred the herbs with a ceramic pestle, all the while reciting incantations for Belasko and his mission, wishing him success.

It was the least that she could do, but there was more.

When she was finished praying, she would make some phone calls, try to glean some information from her friends, and maybe, in the process, rally some support.

It was a risky business; no one had to tell her that. Two years ago, a friend had come to Lacroix, complaining of a hex that made his life a living hell. He had been suffering at work, he couldn't sleep, his social life had gone to hell and now his health was failing. Lacroix had spoken to the witch responsible, attempted to negotiate a settlement. When all else failed, she had applied some magic of her own, to lift the hex and grant her friend a measure of relief.

But in the process, she had made a mortal enemy.

The witch responsible for laying on the curse had been a mercenary sort, enlisted by a jilted lover to exact revenge, and while he had no private grudge with Lacroix's acquaintance, any interference with his magic was a personal affront. He had retaliated with a whispering campaign in the New Orleans magical fraternity, and followed up with a barrage of hexes aimed at Lacroix herself. That day a car had leaped the curb and nearly crushed her as she walked to work. A bewildered driver passed the field sobriety exam, explaining to police that ''something'' yanked the steering wheel out of his grasp as he was driving west on Camp Street. No mechanical malfunction could be found in the vehicle, and the driver paid a fine for reckless driving, but the truth was plain to Marianne Lacroix.

The next day, she had paid a visit to the rival witch,

offered her most sincere apologies and heard them all rejected in disdain. Sharp eyes and nimble fingers saved her, picking up a stray hair from the couch on which she sat. That night, she used it to construct an effigy, pronounced the necessary incantations and commenced to pound the doll with a meat-tenderizing mallet.

Thumbnail coverage in the paper blamed an accidental fall for her tormentor's paralyzing injuries.

She called it self-defense.

It was the first and last time she had used the Art to harm another living creature, and it cost her dearly. Lacroix didn't intend to go that route again, but there were steps that she could take to keep Belasko safe. Philippe Bouchet was dangerous on many levels, but there was no reason why he should discover Lacroix's attempt to block his power.

Not if she was careful.

If she gave herself away somehow, well, she would deal with that threat when it came.

For now, her thoughts and prayers were with Belasko, hunting for a serpent in the dark.

6

The talk with Marianne Lacroix had motivated Bolan to revise his plans. Instead of trying to promote a shooting war between the Dixie Mafia and Haitian posse, he decided to eliminate the redneck leadership as expeditiously as possible, then concentrate on wiping out the voodoo syndicate, which seemed to constitute a greater long-term threat.

It wasn't magic that concerned him, but the ruthlessness Philippe Bouchet and company had already displayed in their attempt to seize control of the Louisiana drug trade. Other, smaller Haitian gangs were already at work in Florida, along the Gulf Coast, and if Bouchet was victorious in his attempt to grab New Orleans from the Dixie Mafia, he would become a role model for the others, possibly annexing them into a larger and more deadly syndicate.

A killing blow against Bouchet's opponents would appear to help the Haitian's cause, but Bolan had his reasons for beginning with a mop-up of the other side. For one thing, he didn't want Doobie Arnold's men distracting him while he was busy with the voodoo posse, striking from his blind side when he needed focus, concentration, to survive. Likewise, there was a chance that he wouldn't survive the battle with Bouchet, and Bolan didn't like to leave a job half-finished. If he had the option to decapitate the Dixie Mafia, kill two snakes with a single stone, it would have been ridiculous for him to pass up the opportunity.

A preliminary bout, then, warming up his muscles for

the main event. He knew that Arnold had a hideout on the north shore of Lake Pontchartrain, west of Slidell, where he would go to ground from time to time, when he was feeling heat from periodic cycles of reform in local government. Nobody bugged him there, either figuratively or literally, but the place was under surveillance by DEA spotters, who reported Arnold's check-in time as half-past noon that very day. He was accompanied by Elva Matthews, his second-in-command, and some two dozen men, armed to the teeth.

Aerial photographs showed Bolan that the hardsite would be difficult to approach by daylight from the landward side, and even darkness wouldn't guarantee success. As for the lakefront, it was guarded from a distance, lookouts watching from the house until the sun went down, one sentry walking an erratic beat that took him past the dock and boathouse every hour or ninety minutes, as the spirit moved him. Arnold and his soldiers clearly felt that any major threat would come at them over the parish roads, in crew wagons or squad cars, but they hadn't reckoned on a visit from the Executioner.

He had to buy some scuba gear, but that was no great problem in a city like New Orleans, situated as it was between the Mississippi River and Louisiana's largest lake. He bought a wet suit, harness, regulator, rubber booties, fins and face mask with a built-in snorkel. Most sport divers rented air tanks, and he had to make three stops before he found a set for sale, topped off and ready to get wet. His final acquisition was a kind of waterproof rubber duffel that had enough room to contain his hardware for the strike.

Then all he had to do was sit and wait for dusk. Aside from sitting on his hands and killing time, the hardest part of Bolan's final preparation was the search for a secluded piece of shoreline where he could begin his swim without an audience of locals standing by to strip his car as soon as he submerged. He found his spot ten minutes after sundown and drove down to the water on a rutted track that ran through chest-high weeds.

Bolan left his street clothes in the car and suited up, then checked out the contents of his underwater tote bag to make sure he had forgotten nothing. He was roughly two miles west of Arnold's private dock, but the surveillance photographs suggested there were better, closer places where a swimmer could negotiate a landing if he had the nerve.

The wet suit fit him like a second skin and kept him warm as he submerged. Once he was back ashore, the jet black Lycra material would replace his normal blacksuit for nocturnal forays, helping him to merge with shadows as he made his move. The rubber duffel bag contained a tube of war paint for his face and hands, assuming he had time to put it on. As for the hardware, he had packed an Uzi submachine gun, the Beretta 93-R, extra magazines for both, six frag grenades and several C-4 plastic charges in a canvas fanny pack, their detonators segregated in a separate pouch. The knife strapped to his right calf would serve well enough for any close-up work, if Bolan met his adversaries hand to hand.

He stuck close to the shoreline, navigating by the bulk of land off to his left as he swam eastward, counting minutes in his head and estimating distance. When he surfaced for the first time, thirty minutes later, he could see the silhouette of Doobie Arnold's boathouse, still some eighty yards ahead. He checked the shore for sentries, found his own mark close at hand and swam in toward the shore.

This was the tricky part, when he was most exposed, with nothing but a knife at hand if someone jumped him from the darkness. Smooth rocks were piled up at the water's edge, as if some landscaper had gone overboard designing a potential picnic spot, and Bolan took advantage of their cover as he hauled himself ashore.

There were no shouts of warning, nothing so far to suggest he had been seen. In seconds flat, he shed his tanks and harness, stashing them between two massive rocks, and eased open the plastic zipper on his underwater bag. The smell of gun oil reached his nostrils, cutting through the slightly brackish odor of the lake.

He smeared his face and hands with war paint, extra camouflage, buckled on his web belt, shrugged into the shoulder holster and looped the bandolier of extra magazines across his chest. The Uzi was already cocked, with a live round in the chamber, and he double-checked the sound suppressor before he eased off the safety.

All systems go.

The Executioner moved toward his target, merging with the shadows of the night.

PHILIPPE BOUCHET HAD many eyes and ears. Wherever true believers served Damballah in New Orleans and environs, he was known and feared. If he required a certain piece of information from the streets, he merely had to ask. Or sometimes, a total stranger would attempt to curry favor with the premier *houngan* in the state by offering some juicy secret of his own accord. In this way, he had learned about a certain "Christian" in the city government whose fondness for pornography involving children made him ripe for blackmail. Thus had Bouchet heard of the police lieutenant in Metairie, whose young wife played bedroom games with black men while her husband was at work.

And so, that afternoon, Bouchet had learned of Marianne Lacroix.

He recognized the name, of course. She ran one of a dozen shops around New Orleans where practitioners of magic could obtain their ritual supplies. Philippe Bouchet had never patronized her store, and while her name was in his mental file, she meant no more than letters scribbled on a page.

Why should a woman and a perfect stranger wish him harm?

Bouchet ran through his memory in search of motives. After fifteen minutes' concentration, he was sure that he had never crossed the woman's path. He hadn't hired, done business with or killed her man, as far as he could tell. He owned no property adjoining hers, and they were not competitors in trade. If she or any member of her family bought drugs from one of his street dealers, it would be a frail connection at the very best.

What motive could she have, then, for inquiring after Bouchet's business deals? It was a new pursuit, he realized, or else he would have heard about her questions earlier. Was it a sinister coincidence that she had started making queries in New Orleans on the same day that his men were attacked and slain by unknown enemies?

Bouchet dismissed the notion with a snarl that made the men staring at his back exchange swift glances, frowning to themselves. It was a bad sign when he started to growl. All of them knew that, and they had witnessed frenzied acts of violence that sometimes went along with Bouchet's sound effects. He was unarmed, as far as any one of them could tell, but that wouldn't prevent his picking up a chair and hurling it across the room, or maybe summoning his soldiers from the waiting room outside, demanding that somebody should be killed.

Instead, Bouchet stopped growling, spoke to no one in particular as he kept staring out the window of his fourth-floor office.

"Who says this again?" he asked.

Louis Germaine spoke up. "A small-time *mambo* in the Quarter," he replied. "Her name's Mama Lois. She's known this Lacroix woman years and years, she says. First time she ever heard a word come out her mouth about our business."

"She say why?"

"No idea, she says. That Mama Lois doesn't like lettin' on that she knows us. All the same, she passed the word on like she was supposed to."

"Makes me wonder why she's askin' now. Somebody wonder that, besides me?"

"I thought about that," Germaine replied.

"You better had thought of that, all three of you. You're no good to me if you aren't thinkin'."

"It could be a coincidence," Germaine stated.

"I don't believe in coincidence," Bouchet growled.

"Me, neither." Germaine glared at the others, daring them to laugh or even smile.

"She might know somethin'," Octave Cuvier put in.

"Now that's a thought." Bouchet turned from the window, facing them. "How could we find that out?"

"Why don't we ask her?" Étienne Ferrau was frowning as he spoke, as if the question taxed him greatly.

Bouchet clapped his hands and aimed an index finger at Ferrau. "You see? Just like that, there's an answer to this problem. We go ask the woman why she's so curious about our business, and if I don't like the answer, then you guys get a chance to ask her."

"I'll pick her up," Germaine said, rising to his feet.

"*They* get her," Bouchet corrected him, with a sharp nod toward Cuvier and Ferrau. "We need to talk some business, while they're at it."

The two men were rooted to their chairs for several seconds more, until Bouchet asked, "Are you still here?"

"We'll get the woman," Cuvier assured him.

"Alive, I mean," Bouchet reminded him. "She's no good to me dead. We need to have a talk first."

"Live it is," Cuvier replied, moving toward the door with Ferrau on his heels.

When they were gone, Bouchet sat beside his second-in-command. "The woman may know somethin', but she didn't do this killin', Louis. Someone else did that."

"I hear you."

"Then you hear me say I want these bastards. Every one of them. If Arnold's white trash got a part in this, we sort them out, right quick."

"I don't see Doobie pullin' a stunt like this. Ask you to a sit-down, maybe, and then have someone jump out of the closet would be more his style."

"Don't let that face and belly fool you, Louis. Doobie Arnold got somethin' up here—" Bouchet's blunt index finger tapped his skull "—or else he'd have been dead a long time ago."

"So, how do you think this sister got involved with Doobie's shit? His people don't like blacks, the way I heard."

"She's black?" Bouchet was startled by the news.

"I told you that, Philippe."

"Just now you told me, Louis. Why didn't I hear that right away, up front?"

Germaine looked troubled. If Bouchet blew, there would be no one to absorb the brunt of it, no one to hide behind.

"I didn't think," he answered, almost whispering.

"You think next time, okay?" Instead of striking him, Bouchet sat back and folded his hands in his lap. "I need to ask her things, no matter what she looks like."

"That's what I thought, too."

"Oh, so you thinkin' now?"

Germaine shut up. He couldn't win.

"The woman either knows who shot up my people, or else she doesn't know. If she doesn't know, there's some other reason she's askin' folks about my game today of all days. Am I right?"

"You're right, Philippe."

"Damned right, I'm right. She must know somethin', either way. I'm going to find out what she knows and make her wish she never stuck her nose where it didn't belong."

And, Bouchet thought, if it turned out the woman knew

nothing whatsoever, he would teach her anyway. A stranger didn't ask about Philippe Bouchet behind his back, not even on a passing whim. That was a lesson all New Orleans stood to learn, within the next few months. The sooner everyone absorbed that simple fact, the safer they would be.

But in the meantime, someone had his sights on Bouchet's men, and by extension, that meant he—or they—meant grave harm to Bouchet, as well. They hadn't reckoned on Damballah, though, and that would be their last mistake.

The Great Serpent would look out for his own and feed upon his enemies.

Philippe Bouchet was looking forward to the feast.

"I DON'T LIKE HIDING," Doobie Arnold groused.

"A little break from business, that's all," Elva Matthews told him. "You know how it goes."

"A little break, my ass. You know who pulled this shit as well as I do. What I *should* be doin' right now, is kicking his black ass back to Haiti."

"And we will," Matthews said. "But it makes no sense to jump the bastard when he's waitin' for it, right? Much better if we take him by surprise. That's how we ought to do it."

"I don't know."

Another crumpled beer can clanked into the half-filled garbage bag, and Arnold reached down toward the ice chest set between the two men, on the patio. His view of Pontchartrain was limited in the darkness, but his eyes picked out the blaze of light that was New Orleans, on the southern shore.

He missed the flash of the explosion, since he was bending down to grab another beer, but Arnold heard it plain enough. The shock wave rattled windows in the house behind him, spiked his eardrums with a flash of pain, like he was suddenly descending from tremendous heights without a parachute. His head snapped up in time to see the flaming ruins of the boathouse shower across the yard in front of him. The roof was sailing off across Lake Pontchartrain, a giant flying disk edged in fire, and he sat there, gaping at it, like a child captivated by a fireworks show. He couldn't seem to help himself.

The next thing Doobie Arnold knew, he was down on the concrete, his legs tangled in the lawn chair, with the weight of Elva Matthews pressing down on top of him. He cursed and threw an elbow into Elva's ribs to get him off, then he understood the noises he was hearing weren't just echoes from the blast: they were the sharp snap-crackle-pop of automatic-weapons fire.

"Get off me, goddammit!"

Even bellowing, his own voice sounded small, all stuffy, like he ought to yawn or chew some gum to clear things up. But there wasn't time to think about his stupid ears. Somebody had followed him out to his hideaway, and they were moving on him. Moving on him now!

The one and only thing that he could do was fight.

It never crossed his mind to run, not really. Doobie Arnold knew that running had no end, once you got started. He had run from fights a couple of times, when he was little, but his daddy's belt had sent him back to face the music, win or lose. And Doobie Arnold didn't lose much—never, when it really counted. In his life, so far, he had been shot three times, stabbed twice, so badly that a lesser man would almost certainly have died, and punched so many times he felt like an over-the-hill boxer. He always got back up again and finished it.

The way he meant to now.

"I said, *get off me!*"

He shoved Matthews aside and pushed up on all fours, not standing until he worked out that the autofire was coming from the far side of the house. The one time Arnold didn't wear a gun, he needed one. It went to prove that you should listen to the Boy Scouts: Be Prepared.

He lumbered to his feet and turned back toward the house. Two steps, and he was sprinting, with Matthews laboring behind him to keep up. The tall glass sliding doors were closed to keep the air-conditioning inside, and Arnold had his hands stretched out in front of him to grab the handle, slide the door back on its runners. He felt goose bumps on his arms as the refrigerated air made contact with his sweaty skin.

He kept guns everywhere around the house, in case of an emergency like this, but where exactly was the closest one? It hit him, and Arnold veered toward the couch, going down on one knee, reaching underneath it for the stubby riot shotgun lying hidden there.

Okay.

He felt a little better now. At least the bastards wouldn't find him waiting empty-handed when they came for him. Assuming any of them got that far.

But waiting didn't suit him. He was angry, more at being frightened in his own backyard than at the fact of an attempt upon his life. People had been trying to kill Doobie Arnold since he turned sixteen, but he was still around. Still kicking.

Still the boss.

"Let's go," he said to Matthews, moving back in the direction of the fight.

A NEW YORK LANDLORD would have advertised the small apartment as a studio, but Marianne Lacroix was satisfied to call it what it was: a tiny dump that she had sanitized and customized, spruced up and made her own. She had been lucky to locate an older building, with a courtyard in the middle and apartments all around. It was nothing special, but she fixed it up with plants and candles, doting on the fact that it was old, by local standards. There were problems with the plumbing every now and then, but it had soul, a sense of history.

This night, though, Lacroix was wishing that she had checked into a downtown hotel, with a doorman on the street, perhaps a burly house detective prowling through the halls, bright lights and people to surround her, so she wouldn't have to be alone. She had almost surrendered to the impulse, even knowing it was futile, but she finally decided it was best to wait at home, on more familiar ground.

The worst part about prayers, in any faith, was that you never really knew if you would get an answer. More specifically, there was no way of telling just what kind of answer it might be. The story of the monkey's paw came readily to mind and brought a shiver to her spine.

Be careful what you wish for, little girl.

Her grandma used to say that, in the old days, back when she was teaching Marianne the basics of the Art. A prayer or incantation, even simple wishing, could unleash dynamic forces that would find a way to turn around and attack you if you weren't in firm control of your emotions, the environment, every little thing.

And when you thought about it, who was ever really in control? She did her best and took her chances. That was all. The best that anyone could do.

She had a mental flash of Mike Belasko, vague and nonspecific. Just his face, like in a portrait, but the background was all smoke and fire. She didn't know what he was up to at the moment, but the radio and television news reports were fairly clear on where he'd been before he stopped off at the Silver Chalice for a little chat.

He was some kind of warrior, that one. It was in his eyes, the way he moved, the tenor of his voice. Just looking at him made her warm inside and chilled her all at once. She didn't normally react that way to strangers, men in general, but he was...different.

She hoped that he was still alive.

As for herself, she had already taken various precautions to defend herself in case something went wrong. She had black candles burning, for protection, garlic on the door and windows, with a sprinkling of salt across the threshold. That would stop a *zombi,* she was told, though she had never tried it for herself.

If all else failed, she had the nickel-plated Smith & Wesson Model 65—the so-called Ladysmith—on her coffee table, loaded with .38-caliber hollowpoints. It looked incongruous beside her untouched glass of chardonnay.

She didn't feel like drinking, but she needed something for her nerves. The meditation wasn't helping much, the more she thought of Belasko, out there in the dark. Was he alone? She guessed that he would be a solitary fighter, do his best to keep from dragging anybody else into his war.

But now she was involved. It had been risky, casting spells on his behalf, more risky still to ask her friends about Philippe Bouchet, in search of information she could use to help Belasko.

There was a chance Bouchet might not discover her involvement, but she didn't like the odds. He was a man of power, all her friends agreed—those who would speak of him at all—a man of evil power, who enjoyed his hold on others, bending them to do his will, breaking the few who dared defy him.

Such men were dangerous without the Art. When they possessed it, they were doubly so. The Art was neutral; it responded equally to any skilled practitioner, regardless of his or her motives. Natural laws were invoked, as immutable as gravity or the change of seasons, waiting only for a firm hand to supply direction. Thus, the Art could heal or kill, impoverish or enrich, grant revelations or conceal dark secrets. Whatever ethics or morality might be involved, they were supplied by those who used the Art for good or evil.

And sometimes, when the power flowed, it was like handling a foreign sports car—or a snake. You needed skill, as well as strength, to keep control. One slip, a moment of distraction, and the Art could spin out of your grasp and take off in some wild and unpredictable direction of its own.

That was the challenge and the thrill.

That was the fear.

She almost missed the noise, so subtle was it, like the faintest scratching sound. It seemed to come from the direction of her bedroom, but she wasn't sure. Old buildings had a symphony of noises all their own.

It would be better to make sure.

She took a sip of wine, picked up the Ladysmith and moved toward the single bedroom. It was dark back there, but Lacroix wouldn't allow her own home to intimidate her. She wasn't a child to jump at shadows, not when she had taken every possible precaution, not when she was armed.

She reached the bedroom threshold, reached in for the light switch and flicked it on. The room was empty, but she took the extra time to check her closet just in case. The .38, although presumably designed for women, still felt heavy in her hand. A glance beneath the bed, and she was out of there—in time to hear the small noise emanating from the bathroom.

The faucet was dripping. But she had to check it out, regardless. Once again, she reached in for the light switch, gasping as a strong hand closed around her wrist and yanked her off her feet, propelled her right across the room.

She felt the plastic shower curtain wrap itself around her like a shroud, then her head struck tile, the shower wall, and she was on her knees. She grappled with the curtain, wincing as the lights came on above her, conscious of a hulking shadow close at hand.

She tried to raise the pistol, felt it twisted from her grasp before she had a chance to aim and fire. It splashed into the toilet bowl, effectively beyond her reach.

A black man towered over her, regarding her with an expression that spoke more of curiosity than rage. She didn't recognize him, but she saw the rawhide thong around his neck, the lump beneath his T-shirt, just above his heart, and knew the mojo bag made him a true believer. Not Bouchet himself, of course; the *houngan* wouldn't deign to run an errand of this kind. He had disciples standing by to do his dirty work.

Her mind went blank, the incantations suddenly deserting her. She couldn't reach the gun, had no hope in the world of overpowering this man. The open window just above her head told Lacroix how he had slipped into the flat, but there was no way she could reach it and escape before he grabbed her, dragged her back.

If this man meant to kill her, she was dead.

A mocking smile lit up his face.

"Time for you to come with me," he said. "We got a little party goin' on."

THE UZI STUTTERED, spewing half a dozen parabellum rounds, and Bolan watched his target go down thrashing on the grass. More guns were coming, homing on the sounds of combat, but he didn't plan to wait for them and make himself a sitting duck.

He primed a frag grenade and lobbed it toward the sound of voices, shadow-shapes advancing in a clutch across the wide, dark lawn, already moving by the time the high-explosive charge went off and screams replaced the shouted questions as shrapnel hissed through the night.

He sprinted toward the house, felt someone moving on his left and swung in that direction with the Uzi, squeezing off a burst before he had clear target acquisition. He got lucky, saw the shooter lurch and stagger, going down with arms and legs outflung. Alive or dead, it didn't matter, just

as long as he was out of action for the moment, letting
Bolan pass.

All kinds of guns were going off around him, none with
any clear fix on their target, but it helped a man to do
something in that kind of situation, waste a few rounds if
he had to, just to feel that he was in the game, not waiting
for the Reaper to reach out and slap him down. Some of
the bullets whispered close enough to make the Executioner
duck his head and veer off course, while others sliced the
darkness yards away from him, wasted on the night.

He ran as if his life depended on it, knowing that his
mission did. His opening diversion with the boathouse was
a fading memory by now, eclipsed by shifting action.
Doobie Arnold waited for him, somewhere in the house or
on the shadowed grounds, and Bolan had to find him soon
if he was going to succeed with this phase of his blitz. The
longer he delayed, the greater chance he had of being shot
down by the palace guard or cornered at the scene when
sheriff's deputies began to arrive in response to panicked
phone calls from the neighbors.

Bolan reached the house, ducked underneath a lighted
window, looking for a way inside. There was a door in
front of him, another twelve or thirteen paces. He focused
on it, gaining ground as it began to open and armed men
stepped out into the night.

The pointman turned and spotted him as Bolan skidded
to a halt on recently-mowed grass. Some kind of automatic
rifle glinted in the moonlight, rising in the shooter's hands,
and the Executioner let the Uzi rip, no time to aim as instinct called the play. His bullets ripped a zigzag course
across the open door, made someone squeal behind it,
tracking on to catch the pointman in the chest and throat.
He went down firing from the hip, his aim spoiled by the
impact of 9 mm bullets striking flesh and bone, his rifle
kicking free of lifeless fingers after spraying ten or fifteen
rounds at the moon.

The Executioner advanced behind another burst of automatic fire, hosing the doorway with a stream of death, the last man of a trio sprawling facedown on the prostrate body of his fallen comrades. It was clear, and Bolan was prepared to move inside, when shouted words demanded his attention, tugging at a corner of his mind.

"Yo, Doobie! Wait up, man!"

He swiveled toward the voice, saw two men running hard for the detached garage, a chunky third man laboring to overtake them. Bolan couldn't see their faces, but he reckoned there could only be one Doobie at the hardsite, even in a world of Billy Bobs and Bubbas.

It was now or never, do or die.

He ran for the garage, thigh muscles burning in the sprint. Ahead of him, the fat boy had to have sensed impending danger somehow, breaking stride and turning back to face the house. He gaped at Bolan, cursing, leveling a sawed-off shotgun as he braced himself to fire.

It didn't take a marksman to score hits at that range, with a barrel less than sixteen inches long. Bolan was dead, unless he made a move right then. Instinct and years of training took over from his conscious mind. He twisted in midstride, pitched over to his left, and went down in a flying shoulder roll. The shotgun bellowed, sending a swarm of double-aught buckshot buzzing through the space he had occupied a half second earlier. The chunky shooter cursed again and jacked another shell into the scattergun's chamber, pivoting to make up for his first mistake.

He never got the chance, as Bolan's Uzi chattered back at him. A burst of parabellum manglers stitched him from gut to Adam's apple, spinning him off center as he fired a second time. The shotgun blast churned up a mighty divot at his feet, then the redneck crumpled, burying the sawed-off weapon underneath his lifeless bulk.

Bolan was on his feet and moving by the time his adversary fell, mind focused on the long, low shape of the garage. He heard an engine revving up inside, and was ready when the right-hand section of the wooden door burst open, ripped apart by the explosive exit of a Chevy Blazer. Its headlights kicked into high the instant it was clear.

He stood directly in the Blazer's path and switched the Uzi to his left hand, palmed a frag grenade, yanked the pin and released the spoon. He held it as he ticked off the numbers in his head, then lobbed the bomb past the headlights, toward the Blazer's windshield and the men inside the charging vehicle. The Uzi hammered, bullets striking sparks from grille and bumper, peeling strips of paint back on the Blazer's hood.

The frag grenade went off on impact, smoke and fire enveloping the Blazer. Still, it kept on rolling, with a dead man at the wheel, another corpse beside him in the shotgun seat. The driver's foot was jammed on the accelerator, revving the big engine, and the sloping lawn was free of obstacles once Bolan stepped aside to let the flaming hearse roll past.

He watched it racing toward the darkness of Lake Pontchartrain, leaving a trail of smoke and sparks behind it, like some earthbound comet. Only when it reached the brink and disappeared did Bolan glance back toward the house, where the surviving members of the hardforce were collecting for a final charge.

He took advantage of the darkness and confusion, leaving them to wonder what had happened to their boss. It was an easy run back to the boulders where his diving gear was stashed, nobody searching in that direction as he made his getaway.

The troops meant nothing to him, now that they were leaderless. Another Doobie Arnold might emerge from their befuddled ranks one day, but that wasn't his problem at the moment.

Bolan had another adversary waiting for him in New Orleans, and he didn't plan to keep him waiting long.

7

Bolan stopped by the apartment unannounced to visit Marianne Lacroix. The night was getting on, but it wasn't that late, all things considered. He decided to play it by ear and knock if he saw signs of life, pass on if it appeared that she had gone to bed. He had no expectations for the visit, other than to satisfy himself that she was safe, and to discover what—if anything—she might have learned about Philippe Bouchet since they'd last spoken.

He parked outside the complex and a half-block down, walking back through misting rain that barely dampened his hair and jacket. He was lightly armed, with the Beretta 93-R, extra magazines and a stiletto, but he sensed no danger in the neighborhood—at least, no more than would be found in any urban setting after nightfall.

Once inside the complex, with its mock Spanish courtyard and hanging potted plants, he spent a moment scouting out the territory, seeking number 207. It was on the second level, obviously, and he counted backward from 213, just above him, until he spied a set of windows showing light within, through partly opened draperies. The stairs were metal, reminiscent of a fire escape. In thirty seconds, he was standing on the woman's welcome mat—and saw the door ajar.

The 93-R found his hand without a conscious order. Bolan toed the door back several inches farther, widening the slice of Lacroix's small living room that he could see.

Black candles flickered on the coffee table, melted down to three-inch nubs. There was no sign of any living occupant, and Bolan's nerves were screaming at him to hurry, but he forced himself to take his time, first rapping lightly on the door with his Beretta, calling out to Lacroix, proceeding only when she failed to answer him.

The search took all of sixty seconds flat. He found the shower curtain lying tangled on the bathroom floor, ripped from its metal rings, and a .38 revolver soaking in the toilet bowl. There were no other signs of struggle—nothing in the way of blood or broken furniture, for instance—but the absence of a corpse didn't put Bolan's mind at ease. The open bathroom window showed how her abductors had gained entry to the flat, and they had clearly gone out through the front door with their prisoner.

He went back to the living room and closed the door, prepared to make another, longer and more thorough search. The voodoo effigy was staring at him from the backside of the door as Bolan eased it shut: it was a female doll, this time—or so he gathered, from the strands of hair that dangled to the stunted figure's waist. Some kind of cryptic symbol had been painted on the doll's flat chest and abdomen in blood, already dried to the color of rust.

He checked the flat again for further signs of mayhem, came up empty and was reasonably satisfied that Lacroix hadn't been forced to donate *her* blood for the painting of the effigy. It seemed the kind of thing that would be done before the raid, a prefatory ritual of sorts. If all her captors wanted was to kill her, Bolan thought, they could have done the job and left her there, another mute example to their enemies.

And that, in turn, meant there was still a chance, however slim, that he could rescue her alive. The voodoo doll told Bolan that Philippe Bouchet was almost certainly responsible for the abduction. If he hadn't ordered it directly, it was likely that he knew the men responsible and would have been consulted prior to any action being taken.

Either way, the *houngan* graduated to the head of Bolan's hit parade.

But he would need more information than he had in hand to pull it off. And there was only one place he could get it now.

He wiped the telephone for fingerprints when he was done and blew the candles out before he left. The short walk to his Skylark seemed to take forever, but he kept himself from running with a force of will.

The fire was coming, soon enough, and there were some alive this night who would be going up in smoke before the sun went down again.

TOM CARLISLE RECOGNIZED the tension in Belasko's voice, despite the barest trace of static on his cordless telephone. The message had been brief, succinct. A time, location and a simple question: Could he meet Belasko?

As it happened, Carlisle could. He wasn't hanging with the homeys at the moment, working overtime to curry favor with Philippe Bouchet and company. In fact, the whole damned crew—or what was left of it—had gone to ground since the attacks that morning. No one had reached out for Carlisle to consult with him or keep him current on their latest plans. He wasn't that far in, as yet, for them to trust him with last-minute battle plans. They recognized a player hoping for advancement, but the normal give-and-take of business would be put on hold while they were dealing with the unexpected threat from Mike Belasko.

Slipping on a light windbreaker, making sure the Glock was tucked into his waistband, Carlisle still had trouble comprehending that the past few days weren't some kind of waking nightmare. Ferris Burke getting killed that way, like something from a slaughterhouse, and then his field commander sending him Belasko, like some kind of loaded booby prize.

A booby *trap* would be more like it, Carlisle thought as he was walking to his car. There was no sign of any watchers on the street, but he would take precautions anyway, to satisfy himself. He still had almost fifteen minutes, for a six- or seven-minute drive to the Girod Street Wharf. That should be ample time to spot and lose a tail, in the event—unlikely, he admitted to himself—that he was being watched.

In fact, no cars pulled out behind him as he drove away, but Carlisle kept the promise to himself and made a winding circuit of the Quarter, coming back on Water Street, southbound, the opposite direction from his starting point. The traffic would have helped a shadow in the Quarter, but it was improbable, to say the least, that anyone would wait that long to pick him up. If they hadn't been waiting at his flat, he should be free and clear.

Which made him wonder if Belasko was the same.

The guy was smart enough to know you didn't make contact when you're being tailed, but what if he was tagged, somehow, and didn't know it? Carlisle didn't buy that voodoo shit, but there were countless stories circulating through New Orleans—*black* New Orleans, anyway— about Philippe Bouchet, his posse and the powers they were rumored to possess. You couldn't swing a dead cat out in Terrytown without hitting someone who knew someone else, a friend of a friend of a friend, who was cursed by Bouchet or rewarded by magic for some trifling act of respect. The curses were always more interesting: a water moccasin in the bathtub; spiders in the bed; a brother vanished, with a voodoo doll left in his place. Most of the incidents could be explained by simple logic, but they had a cumulative weight among superstitious Haitians, and for a surprising number of native-born homeys, as well.

He found a parking place and left the car, kept watching

out for shadows as he moved in the direction of the wharf.
A couple seafood restaurants would still be open there, but
no great crowds hung out along the wharfs at night. Some
fishermen, perhaps. Maybe a small-time pusher dropping
by for a delivery.

No sweat.

He wore his jacket open, all the same, to allow quick
access to the Glock. Belasko was already waiting for him
when he reached the far end of the wharf.

"What's up, man?"

"Where would Bouchet take a hostage if he wanted
privacy?"

The question startled Carlisle. "All depends," he said,
"on who it is and what he's doing. Can you fill me in?"

Belasko let him have the basics from the top. He didn't
recognize the woman's name, but that was no surprise. He
also wouldn't care to bet his pension on the odds of someone finding her alive, but Carlisle kept the observation to
himself.

"If it was me," he said at last, "I'd want to ask somebody from the posse."

"Anybody in particular?"

"Could be. You want to play this on your own, or
what?"

"I'm open to suggestions."

Carlisle thought about it, measuring the odds and angles.
"If he recognizes me, I'm blown, you know?"

"A name is all I need."

The DEA man shook his head at that. "No, man. You
need a way inside, but you're a little pale."

"So?"

Carlisle hesitated for another moment, thinking of his
partner, but his mind was already made up. "So, nothing,"
he replied. "Fact is, I need a little exercise. I'm tired of
sitting on my ass."

MARIANNE LACROIX experienced a sense of movement, clawing her way back to consciousness with an effort. She was groggy, stuporous. It felt as if someone had packed ten pounds of cotton wool between her ears. The drug was starting to wear off a little, but she still had no idea what they had used to put her out. She could recall the needle vaguely, and a giddy, nauseating feeling as the room began to swim around her. She was swirling with a rush of luke-warm water, down a giant drain, until she woke up... where?

She was inside some kind of motor vehicle—that much was obvious. Her hands were bound behind her with rough twine, her ankles likewise, with her feet and hands connected somehow, so that every time she tried to straighten out her legs, the rough noose tightened on her wrists.

She was hog-tied, and blindfolded as well.

The vehicle was larger than a normal car, more spacious. She had room to shift around on turns, and felt ribbed steel beneath her, rather than the normal carpeting. A van, perhaps? It felt too large for that, and there was no sound from the driver or his other passengers up front.

Some kind of truck, then, she assumed. Bouchet was using a delivery vehicle to transport her, for personal convenience or some other reasons of his own. The bottom line was that she cared less for the mode of transportation than for the intended destination.

Where was Bouchet taking her and why?

The fact that she was still alive was good news and bad news. If the *houngan* simply wanted her eliminated, he could easily have had her killed at home. If he saw fit to carry her away, it had to mean he wanted her alive, for at least a little while.

Same question: why?

Her mind was clear enough by now to make some of the puzzle pieces fit. Bouchet had learned of her attempts to gather information on his gang, which meant that one of those she trusted had to have sold her out. It didn't matter which one had betrayed her at the moment. She had ways of answering that question later...if she lived.

She could think of only two reasons why Bouchet might want her alive. He might desire to question her about her sudden interest in the posse, maybe look for a connection to his recent troubles in New Orleans, or he might intend to use her in a ritual. Of course, the notions weren't mutually exclusive. He could always grill her first, take care that she had life enough remaining to be useful as a sacrifice.

The thought raised goose bumps on her naked arms. It wasn't cold inside the truck, and Lacroix ascribed the sudden chill to fear. She had a fair idea of what Bouchet could do, and there were no illusions about sudden rescue from the clutches of the beast.

Well, there was Belasko, but he didn't even know that she had been abducted, much less where Bouchet was taking her. Assuming he discovered what had happened, Lacroix still recognized that any thought of rescue by a white knight on a charger was the flimsiest of fantasies. Without her tools, or even the ability to move her hands, her magic would be next to useless. She could only hope to find the strength within herself to stand against Bouchet as long as possible, without submitting to the *houngan*'s will.

It was a lost cause, even so. Her pain threshold was relatively high, but Lacroix had never once confused herself with Superwoman. She was terrified right now, and thankful there was no one with her at the moment who would take advantage of her helplessness.

How did she know there was no one else?

The smell. Unconsciously her mind had set about the task of sorting odors, cataloging them. She picked out dust, some kind of motor oil, old rubber, musty cardboard, fear-sweat emanating from herself. If there was anyone else with her in the truck, he had to have been packed inside a vacuum jar.

She wasn't completely helpless, then, she told herself. She had her wits.

And much good they would do her, once Bouchet and his interrogators went to work. How long could she hold out against his magic—or against cold steel—with nerve alone?

Not long.

Her eyes were moist with tears behind the blindfold, but she tried to make her mind a blank, erase the brooding fear. Whatever lay ahead of her, she was alive right now, and that was all that mattered. There was always hope while life remained.

But no one had to tell her that her hope—and life—were running out.

PO' BOYS WAS a strip club on Canal Street in the French Quarter. The dancers, staff, and nine-tenths of the clientele were black, so Bolan waited in the car while Tom Carlisle went in to scout the place and find their pigeon.

They were looking for a Haitian named Mason DuBois, described by Carlisle as a sort of noncom in the local posse, high enough in rank to know of any major plays, but not so lofty that he would be summoned to a meeting of the general staff. He hung out at Po' Boys four or five nights a week, when he wasn't out working for Bouchet. There was a dancer named Cedretta who was said to do him favors now and then, when she was off the clock, and whether it was true or not, the club was well-known as a place where pimps and players came to let themselves be seen, show off their gold and threads or maybe talk a deal.

"If he's not in here, I'll find out if Cedretta's working, run along and check her crib. Or we can try his place, across the river in Gretna. We'll come up with something pretty quick. No sweat."

So Bolan sat and waited.

The heavy, syncopated sounds of rap reached out to Bolan as the door to Po' Boys opened and two men emerged. Tom Carlisle led the way, speaking earnestly to a man who was slightly shorter, but stocky, with a prison-yard weight-lifter's build. The stranger looked around and started to argue with Carlisle, but he didn't pull away as the DEA agent led him toward the Skylark.

"Man, this action better be all that and then some, you know what I'm sayin'?"

"I hear you, brother."

"'Cause my Cedretta's lookin' *fine* tonight, you know what I'm sayin'?"

"This won't take long."

When they were ten feet from the Buick, Bolan showed himself. Mason DuBois blinked once, then shot a sidelong glance at Carlisle, anger and suspicion showing on his face.

"Hey, man, what is this shit? You brought me out of the club to see a white man? You're way out of line, know what I'm sayin'?"

"I know what you're saying, Mason," Carlisle told him. "We just want to have a little talk, that's all."

"Who's we? You with this mother—"

Carlisle slapped him hard across the face. DuBois stepped backward, snarling, reaching underneath his jacket for some kind of hardware. In another moment, he would probably have reached it, but his time ran out as Carlisle stepped in close and drove a fist into his face. The Haitian staggered, one leg buckling under him, a dazed expression on his face. He barely knew it when the Executioner stepped in behind him, locked an arm around his neck and squeezed just hard enough to put him out.

"Remind me not to piss you off," Bolan said as they lugged their burden to the car and put him in the trunk, relieved him of a shiny automatic and a switchblade prior to lowering the lid.

"I'd just as soon have shot him," Carlisle retorted.

"Not yet." They pulled out from the curb, with Bolan at the wheel. "You're sure about this place?"

"Sure as can be," the fed replied. "It's like that movie poster said about the alien—'In space, no one can hear you scream.'"

"I'd rather hear him talk."

"We'll get there, no sweat. This blackbird's going to sing."

"WELCOME TO MY HOME away from home."

Philippe Bouchet enjoyed the apprehension on his captive's face as he removed the blindfold, giving her a first look at her prison cell. It had been necessary to untie her ankles so that she could walk, but even if she bolted now, there was nowhere for her to go.

He had her cold.

"Please, sit." He waved her toward a straight-backed wooden chair, the only piece of furniture in sight.

"I'd rather stand," she said.

"As you prefer...for now." He wore his most ingratiating smile, took pride in his performance as the perfect host. "It was most kind of you to join us."

"Like I had a choice."

"We all got choices. Stand or sit. Stay put or travel. Live or die."

"What do you want from me?"

"I should be askin' you that question. You've been ringin' phones all over town today, inquirin' after me and mine."

"I don't know what you mean," she said.

"Okay. Play dumb if that's the way you want to go. I'm goin' to undertake to change your mind, in just a little while. We'll see, then, what you're made of."

"There's been some mistake," she told him.

"That's the truth. You make a big mistake when you

come sniffin' after me, today of all days. Another time, I might not care so much. I might be flattered, even. Have a fancy piece like you so interested. Thing is about today, I've got all kinds of problems comin' down on me at once, you know? Makes me suspicious when you start callin' folks all over town and ask about my business."

"Honestly, I don't—"

"Be careful now," he interrupted her. "Somebody tells me 'honestly,' I guess the chances are they're about to lie their ass off."

She had no response to that, dark eyes regarding him with fear and curiosity, all mixed up into something else that had no name.

"Do I know you?"

"Not really. No." More definite the second time, as Bouchet stared at her.

"I know your people?"

"No." She faced him squarely, not like she was hiding, saving that for later.

"So, I never did you any dirt. That true?"

Stone silence from the prisoner.

"So why you go askin' people about my business, then? Nobody ever tell you about that stalkin' law we got?"

"Am I under arrest?"

He had to laugh at that, the woman standing right up in his face and talking back to him like she was going to live forever. He admired that kind of spirit, even when it was an obstacle. So far, the *houngan*'s life had been a string of triumphs, obstacles demolished in the face of overwhelming odds. He owed Damballah something, for his luck, but some of it came back to him, as well.

"That's funny. Yeah, you been arrested by the People's Court, okay? The charge is stickin' in your nose where it shouldn't ought to be. Save everybody lots of time if you confess and tell me what I need to know."

"Which is?"

"Who put you on me for a start. What you expect to get from doggin' me. That kind of thing."

"I don't know what you mean."

"Okay, we'll do it your way," he replied. "I think you'll change your mind before we finish, though. I surely do."

"And if I don't?"

"I'm bound to spoil your day. Spoil your whole damned life. When I need answers, there's no way for me to quit till I get answers."

She stared at him in silence, scared but keeping right on top of it so far. He hesitated for a moment, then it hit him, like a slap across the face.

"You think somebody's comin' for you."

"What? No, honest— No. You're wrong."

"That may be. I've been wrong before," he said, "but never much on big things. Tell you what—I'll make a little welcome ready for your friends, in case they do stop by. How'd that be?"

"Suit yourself."

"I will, indeed. I'm goin' to do just that."

IT WASN'T OUTER SPACE, but it was close enough. The river warehouse was deserted, and it stood apart from its surrounding neighbors by some fifty yards. Inside, a full third of the place had been constructed as a giant freezer. You could test-fire rocket launchers in there, with the door closed, and it would be deathly still outside.

Mason DuBois was wearing handcuffs. They fit nicely on the meat hook, dangling overhead, and made him stand on tiptoes. The refrigerator had been disconnected for a long time now, and he was sweating through his silk shirt, watching Bolan, shooting little glances off toward Carlisle on the side.

"I don't know what you're up to, man, but this a bad mistake you makin'."

"Really?"

"Fuckin' A, you're *really* in the shit."

"I'd say it was the other way around," the Executioner replied.

"That's because you don't be thinkin' who I'm with, white man. Why don't you ask your boy over there."

Carlisle stepped in and hit him with a short jab to the kidney, snarling, "'Boy' that, you piece of shit."

"The reason we invited you to have this chat," Bolan said, "is because I know exactly who you work for. He's got something that I want. You're just about to help me get it back."

"Fuck y'all."

"Not likely. Just let me tell you what I need, so we can try to work this out."

"Say what you want, I'll not be—"

Carlisle's right hook to the solar plexus left him breathless, sucking air in like a drowning man.

"As I was saying, Bouchet picked up a woman tonight, named Marianne Lacroix. He's holding her somewhere, could be for questioning. I'm after the location," Bolan said. "You talk, you walk."

"I'll tell you this, white man—your mother was—"

The Glock sprang into Carlisle's hand and slashed across the captive's face. DuBois blinked rapidly to clear his eyes of tears, and when they came back into focus, he was staring down the automatic's barrel.

"Hear this chump, before you say another fuckin' word," Carlisle said. "If it was up to me, I would've smoked you back at Po' Boys, for my partner, got it? Only reason you're alive right now, is for the man to get some answers."

"What partner, man?" Blood flew in little droplets from DuBois's lips as he spoke.

"White man named Ferris Burke. That ring a bell? Y'all snuffed him five, six nights ago."

"You fuckin' DEA, man? You can't pull this kind of shit! I got my rights!"

"You got last rites, if I hear another word somebody didn't ask you for. You want to die right now, say something smart. Say 'please,' you sack of shit."

DuBois kept silent, turning his apprehensive gaze toward Bolan, waiting.

"You know what I want to hear," the Executioner remarked. "One answer pays the tab."

"So, how you know I'm not lyin', man?"

"You've got an honest face."

"What's left of it," Carlisle said.

"And I won't have any trouble finding you, if anything goes wrong."

"Okay, man." Resignation set in. "Philippe got himself this island off the coast there, from Biloxi. Not the big ones. This little speck of nothin' is maybe half a mile from end to end. There ain't no causeway, but he got himself a ferry, like, that can take cars over, if he feel like."

"Let's pin it down," Bolan suggested.

"Not Deer Island, where they got the shrimp and oysters. Farther out than that, a couple miles. Before you get to that Ship Island, where they got the fort and shit."

"I know the place," Carlisle said.

"That's where he took the woman?"

"What he told me," DuBois replied. "If he was lyin' to me, I don't know it."

"Fair enough."

"I'm finished, then?"

He glanced at Carlisle and raised an eyebrow, saw the agent nod.

"Looks like," Bolan said, moving toward the door.

"Hey, where you goin', man?"

"Just stepping out to get some air."

"Hey, man—"

The night was warm out on the warehouse loading dock.

Carlisle joined him moments later, looking grim. "I had to get my cuffs," was all he said.

"You know this place," Bolan said evenly. "If you could point me in the right direction—"

"Nope. I'm coming with you."

"That's not necessary. Your ass is hanging out a mile already."

"Hey, we all got dues to pay," Carlisle commented, moving toward the stairs. "Come on, I'll drive."

8

They switched off the outboard motor and started paddling from three-quarters of a mile offshore. Sound carried over open water, but the Mississippi coast between Gulfport and Pascagoula was a busy shipping area; the Intracoastal Waterway combined with fishing operations and a host of pleasure craft to guarantee that there was always someone on the water, day or night. Unless Bouchet had started posting picket ships, Tom Carlisle was convinced that they could reach the island unobserved.

And what then? Carlisle asked himself. What happened then?

More killing, one way or another.

Carlisle didn't know the woman they were looking for, had never even seen her, but she obviously meant something to Mike Belasko. Carlisle didn't bother asking whether it was duty or a personal connection. He had crossed that line already once himself. Back in the river warehouse, he had passed what he believed might be the point of no return.

Mason DuBois wasn't the first man he had killed. He had two other dead men on his conscience, killed in self-defense on drug raids, but they didn't cost him any sleep at night. DuBois was the first man Carlisle had ever executed in cold blood, and he was troubled by the feeling that he wouldn't lose much sleep over that killing, either.

It was payback, granted, for the torture and slaying of

his partner, and he wasn't even with the posse yet in that regard. Still, there was all the difference in the world between a shooting in the line of duty, even marginal, and putting one between some sorry bastard's eyes while he was dangling by a pair of handcuffs from a meat hook.

Carlisle knew he should be racked with guilt and anguish, but it simply wasn't in him to feel sorry for DuBois. Instead, he found himself imagining Philippe Bouchet framed in his gun sights, throwing up his hands in the belief that it would save him from a copper going by the book.

He felt as if he had been lifted out of time and space the past few hours, maybe zapped into a parallel universe where justice didn't take forever to wind through the courts, and bad guys suffered for their sins instead of laughing as they paid some measly fine and went away to serve a year in minimum security, with MTV and HBO piped into every cell.

He felt as if, just once, he had the chance to put things right.

It went against his training, though, no doubt about it. Even though the brass had teamed him with Belasko, Carlisle had to figure they would shit ten kinds of bricks if they had any clue to what was happening.

But what they didn't know couldn't hurt him.

A little voice at the back of his mind told him not to sweat it, that he probably would be dead the next day anyway.

There was a damned good chance of that, he realized, despite the hardware they were packing, courtesy of Mike Belasko's stash. Assuming Dubois hadn't lied, and Bouchet had the woman on his private island, he would also have an army with him. Carlisle couldn't guess how many hardmen there would be—at least two dozen, maybe more—but they were bad odds any way you broke it down. He thought they would be lucky if the Haitians killed them outright, rather than taking them alive and holding them for some voodoo ceremony.

Still, you couldn't always tell about such things. Belasko had been kicking Doobie Arnold's ass while taking on Bouchet at the same time. It hadn't worked out that well for his girlfriend, granted, but the hard-eyed white man wasn't giving up. Belasko told Carlisle that he would either bring the woman out or settle up the score, and either way it played, Bouchet was picking up the tab.

It sounded fair. Carlisle just hoped that he would be around to join the celebration if Belasko pulled it off.

And if he wasn't, well, he'd always thought old-age retirement was an overrated goal. He might as well go out with style and count for something, rather than put in his thirty and settle for a mobile home in Lauderdale, where he could watch the dope boats cruising up and down the coast.

"Heads up," he said, and pointed to the darker outline of a land mass rising from dark water several hundred yards in front of them. "We're coming up on Bouchet's island hideaway."

And even from that distance, he could hear the drums.

THE FEAR HAD SETTLED in on Marianne Lacroix like something tangible, a weight that bowed her shoulders, made it difficult for her to catch her breath. She had a fair idea of what Bouchet had planned for her and what she could expect to suffer when the ritual began. There might be questions, and she didn't know if she would have the strength of will to keep from babbling everything she knew, but the woman was thankful that her knowledge of Belasko was extremely limited.

The name was very probably an alias, she realized, and while she could describe him for Bouchet, the general description might fit any one of several thousand Crescent City men...until you saw his eyes.

They were a hunter's eyes, she thought, and news reports had borne her out on that score, ticking off the carnage in New Orleans and the suburbs when Belasko went to work on his appointed enemies. Bouchet was on that list, up near the top, and Lacroix found solace in the knowledge that his time was coming. She would almost certainly be dead before it happened, but Bouchet wouldn't be far behind her.

It shocked her, even now, to find that she could wish a stranger dead—not only dead, but suffering before he died—and feel no guilt about it. She wasn't a violent woman, but Philippe Bouchet was evil. He had ruined countless lives, between his magic and the drugs he sold. Before much longer, he would end *her* life, and Lacroix had no illusion that the *houngan* would permit her to die mercifully. And so, she thought, it would be nice to watch him die—if not a pleasure, then at least a feeling of relief that one more human predator had been eliminated from the world.

She listened to the drums and wondered how much time was left before they came for her. She had attended voodoo ceremonies in New Orleans half a dozen times, but none like this. The rare *houngans* who practiced human sacrifice remained at large by taking strict security precautions, limiting attendance at their ceremonies to a trusted few disciples, typically disposing of the evidence with special care. In one respect, she knew it was a privilege of sorts to witness the clandestine ritual, but Marianne Lacroix would happily have passed the "honor" by.

How long?

She wasn't all that desperate to know the answer when she came right down to it, but it was difficult to think of anything else. She had an inkling now of how it had to feel to walk out of a doctor's office with your own death warrant scribbled out on a prescription pad.

That kind of news was handed out to several thousand people every day, while others blundered into death without a hint of warning. Stepping off the curb to cross a street or slipping in the shower, maybe trimming branches from that shade tree near the power lines.

To know, or not to know?

Now that she had the personal experience of knowing she would die, and roughly how it would occur, she was prepared to cast her vote in favor of surprise. You didn't have a chance to put your life in order that way, but it was more merciful—a lightning strike, stray bullet or a speeding taxicab. Anticipating death was worse than crossing over to the other side. It had to be.

She stiffened at the sound of footsteps, felt the ice-cold spike of panic as they stopped outside her door and someone keyed the lock. Philippe Bouchet walked in, with three goons close behind him. They were grinning at her, as if she were dinner and they hadn't eaten for a week.

"We're ready for you. May I call you Marianne?"

"If I say no?"

"You right." The *houngan* chuckled. "It don't mean shit to me."

He nodded, and the thugs closed in on Lacroix. She thought of fighting them, but there was only so much she could do with bare feet, hands secured behind her back. It struck her as more dignified, somehow, to let them lead her from the cell without a screaming brawl that would inevitably have the same result.

Outside, the night was cool, but with a tropic feel about it. She still didn't know exactly where they were, but it had ceased to matter.

"Fix her up," Bouchet commanded, and the goons on either side of the woman propelled her toward a bonfire that was blazing on the edge of what appeared to be a compound, with bungalows arranged in a rectangular formation and a hundred yards of bare ground in the middle. Lacroix was nearly carried by her escorts, strong hands fastened on her arms and dragging her along so that she barely had a chance to walk.

She had a glimpse of men assembled near the bonfire, something like an altar backlit by the leaping flames, and felt her stomach knot in fear. It was too late for any sort of real resistance, but she felt the panic welling up inside her, urging her to do something, anything, when one of the buildings behind her exploded, and the night dissolved into wild screams.

THE C-4 NEVER FAILED. It was a great attention-getter, under almost any circumstances, and it kicked in with the right amount of shock value to give the underdogs a fighting chance. Bolan touched the blast off from a distance, with a remote detonator, then pivoted to key a second blast across the compound before the echoes of the first one had begun to fade.

They had been lucky, coming in. No one had spotted them as they approached the island, beached their boat and made their way ashore. The drums gave them a point of reference, leading Bolan onward, even though Carlisle had never set foot on the island and he didn't have a clue as to specifically where Bouchet's home away from home was located.

At that, they found the place in record time. There had been sentries posted, but they didn't seem to think much of their job, some kind of milk run ordered on the *houngan*'s whim. The lookouts died, one after another, without raising an alarm to those remaining in the compound. Bolan killed two with his Ka-bar fighting knife, a swift, strong slash across each throat, and Carlisle dropped the other two with single rounds from his sound-suppressed Uzi submachine gun.

Simple.

Checking out the compound took a bit of time, with preparations for a ceremony under way. A bonfire had been lit at one end of the clearing, and members of the posse were milling about in an apparent state of agitation, all stripped to the waist, their chests and faces painted with cryptic designs in a variety of colors. Bolan didn't miss the altar, and he understood its purpose in the present frame of reference.

He tried to figure out which bungalow contained the prisoner, and finally he settled on the largest of the buildings situated at the north end of the compound. Guards were posted there, while other bungalows were left unwatched. It stood to reason that Bouchet would have the biggest, finest dwelling on the island, and it wouldn't be unnatural for him to keep his captive close at hand. It would facilitate interrogation and whatever else he had in mind, without uprooting any of the gunmen from their quarters in the small community.

With that in mind, he placed charges on two buildings on the south side of the central square, then made his way around, detouring past the bonfire, to take up his post across the compound on the other side. Carlisle had the altar covered, hanging back some thirty paces in the tangled forest, waiting for the signal that would let him open fire.

Carlisle had managed his new role so far without a hitch. It was impossible to guess what might be going on inside his head, but he had killed three times without batting an eye, and Bolan had no doubt that he would do his best in a few minutes.

He knew that it wouldn't be long, because the drummers—three of them, supporting heavy wooden drums on shoulder straps—would soon exhaust themselves. They were already sweating freely, whether from exertion and the temperature or something else, he couldn't say. From the expressions on their faces, glassy eyes and sagging lower jaws, he would have bet the mint that they were stoned on ganja or some other drug of the variety employed by some occultists to assist them in summoning gods and demons. Either way, the three musicians were unarmed and would present no serious resistance when the shooting started.

The remainder of the pack didn't appear to be hopped up on anything except their own excitement and anticipation, though he couldn't rule out drugs or alcohol—rum being one of voodoo's leading sacraments—across the board. In fact, he would prefer if some or all of them were slightly wasted. It would slow reaction times and make their aim unsteady with the pistols some of them were wearing or the few long guns he could see lined up against the north wall of the building closest to the bonfire.

Bolan settled in to wait, convinced that Marianne Lacroix had to be the guest of honor for the ritual Bouchet had planned. Things wouldn't get that far, if Bolan had his way, but he wasn't prepared to start a firefight raging while the lady's status and precise location were unknown.

He waited three more minutes, sweating through his tiger-stripe fatigues, before the front door opened on the largest house downrange, and the *houngan* appeared. Behind him, two men carried Marianne Lacroix between them, barely giving her a chance to walk across the hard-packed dirt. A fourth man, bringing up the rear, was taller than the rest, his height exaggerated by the top hat on his head. His face was painted bone white, like a skull, in contrast to the hat and black frock coat he wore. The fat snake draped across his shoulders was a red-tailed boa, harmless, six or seven feet in length.

The perfect Baron Samedi.

Bolan keyed his charges when the small procession reached the middle of the compound, knowing Carlisle had to have seen them coming. When the C-4 blew, he had a glimpse of Baron Samedi lurching sideways, dropping to one knee, the boa panicking and throwing a tight loop around his neck. The two goons holding Lacroix weren't about to let her slip away, although they reached for pistols with their free hands, turning with their captive toward the pair of bungalows that had collapsed in flames. Bouchet himself was staring at the wreckage, shouting something to his people in patois.

As Bolan sighted down the Colt Commando's barrel, Carlisle opened fire on posse members gathered near the bonfire, raking them with parabellum manglers from his Uzi.

All hell broke loose.

PHILIPPE BOUCHET WAS dumbstruck when the bungalows went up in smoke. He had prepared himself for the eventuality of someone tracking down his prisoner by posting guards around the compound. Only four of them, but they were handpicked from among his best, as Bouchet understood the concept. How could anyone have crept in close enough to lob grenades into the compound, much less plant explosive charges in the bungalows?

He started shouting orders to his men in bastard French, the language of his faith and family. The two who held his prisoner already had their guns out, and were staring at the blasted bungalows. His men around the bonfire and the altar had begun to scramble for their weapons, knowing instantly that this wasn't part of the ritual.

Bouchet was snapping at the two men holding Lacroix, demanding that they follow him, when one of them exploded. Rather, it would be more accurate to say his *head* blew up, a fist-sized chunk of skull airborne to parts unknown as the big man toppled forward on his face.

Too slow for shrapnel, Bouchet thought, and even as his mind processed the notion, Marianne Lacroix's surviving guard was hit between the shoulder blades, blood gouting from the wound as he dropped to his knees, then buckled over, sprawling on his back.

The woman saw her chance and bolted, running back in the direction she had come from, breaking stride to land a solid kick on Baron Samedi's jaw as she passed. Preoccupied with breathing, grappling with the boa coiled about his neck, the big man was immediately thrown off balance, rolling in the dirt.

Bouchet considered running after her before he realized that someone *else* was also firing now, with a machine gun, from the general direction of the bonfire. Swiveling in that direction, Bouchet saw a couple of his men go down, and realized that it was time to get away from there as rapidly as possible.

But where to go? With the explosions, shooting, bonfire, general chaos all around him, he couldn't see muzzle-flashes from the hostile weapons, had no way of knowing if his camp was totally surrounded. Two or three good snipers could sow panic in a larger force, and he wasn't prepared to run away if he could win the fight. Conversely, if the enemy was all around him, possibly outnumbering his troops, the only thing for him to do *was* run, escape and live to fight another day.

Bouchet's confusion lasted for perhaps a second and a half, no longer. In the time it took to formulate the thought, his feet were moving, sprinting for the nearest bungalow in hopes that it would cover his retreat. As for escaping from the island, he would have to take it one step at a time.

Dead men weren't much on traveling, the *houngan* knew, but he was still alive and meant to stay that way. The woman didn't matter, even though she could identify him as her kidnapper. Bouchet had ways of reaching out for witnesses in custody, but first he had to clear the scene, prevent himself from being killed or taken prisoner.

And he would need a weapon.

One of his men came running toward him, calling out his name and brandishing a shotgun overhead. Bouchet didn't break stride until he saw the runner stumble, groping backward with his free hand toward the bullet that had bored into his back. He went down, flailing with both arms, his shotgun spinning free of fingers that had surrendered their ability to grip.

Bouchet veered far enough off course to scoop up the weapon, then kept on going. He didn't look back to see if his man was alive or dead. It was a hard world, where only the strongest survived.

And Bouchet meant to be among the living when the sun rose on another day.

THEY HAD AGREED that Carlisle should remove the Uzi's sound suppressor once he was in position, covering the posse members near the bonfire. When it hit the fan, Belasko wanted noise and then some, plenty of confusion to keep Bouchet's people guessing, ducking, running around like the proverbial headless chickens.

No pun intended, Carlisle told himself, and fired another Uzi burst into the scrambling mob downrange. He had dropped several of them, saw them fall, and was surprised again to note that he had no more feeling for them than if he were hunting quail.

No, scratch that. Quail were innocent; men hunted them for food or sport, like blasting eight-ounce birdies with a 12-gauge proved you were a man. *These* human animals were dangerous, a blight on everything and everyone they touched.

And they deserved to die.

He had a mental image of the proverbial book gone up in smoke, the DEA brass throwing up their hands, but he kept firing until the Uzi's bolt locked open on an empty chamber, then he switched the magazines and started in again.

So many targets, and so little time.

He couldn't see the woman or Bouchet, but his last glimpse had shown them running off in opposite directions, while the woman's escorts took a dive. Belasko's work, no doubt. The skull-faced sucker in the top hat lay flat on his back, blank eyes staring at the sky, the snake still wrapped around his neck like a fat, scaly muffler.

Poetic justice.

Several of the posse men had found their weapons, either drawing pistols from their belts or scrambling for the long guns stacked against the nearest bungalow. He couldn't stop them all at once, and some of them were starting to return fire now, albeit without taking time to aim. The bullets sizzled overhead and to left and right, still off the mark, but Carlisle knew that he would have to move, and soon, before they found the range.

He lobbed a hand grenade in the direction of the voodoo altar, shifting his position even as it detonated, spewing shrapnel, dropping one or two of Bouchet's men. He wasn't keeping score, but figured he would know when they were done, unless they killed him first.

That was still possible, now that the first surprise was past, and they were starting to regroup, get organized for mutual defense. There had been something like two dozen gunmen gathered at the bonfire when the shooting started, and the DEA man guessed that he had wasted eight or nine. They weren't all dead, perhaps, but down and out of action for the moment, anyway. Still, that left at least fifteen hostile guns, along with any slackers who were tardy getting to the party.

Even fifteen guns could do it, Carlisle realized. No question there. It took only one bullet, and with fifteen pistols, shotguns, even automatic weapons blasting at him, he would need some freaking magic of his own to keep from going down.

Or maybe he should just get mean.

Bouchet's men were off balance, fighting for their lives, albeit on familiar ground. As for Tom Carlisle, he had written off whatever people thought of as a "normal" life when he had snuffed Mason DuBois back at the river warehouse. That was payback, for his partner, and he wasn't finished yet. Until Philippe Bouchet was stretched out at his feet, he still had all the motivation that he needed to keep fighting, killing anything that moved.

He pitched another hand grenade, this time directly toward the bonfire. When it blew, one whole side of the carefully constructed blaze erupted like a small volcano, flinging timbers, sparks and dancing flames for twenty feet or more. One of the voodoo gunners went down, screaming, with a burning beam across his naked chest, none of his comrades interested enough in risking life and limb to help him free himself.

So fry, Carlisle thought as he found a new mark for the Uzi, three of Bouchet's men circling toward his left, in the direction of the tree line, either hoping they could get around behind him or intent on bailing out to save themselves. Whatever, Carlisle didn't plan to let them get away with it.

He led the pointman by a foot or so, his index finger taking up the Uzi's trigger slack. The SMG spit half a dozen rounds and dropped his human target, thrashing, facedown in the dirt. The other two broke ranks at that, one making for the trees, his partner turning back in the direction of the bungalows. But Carlisle caught them both, stitching a figure eight that left them stretched out on the ground, within a few short paces of their friend.

That meant that he had cut the hostile odds roughly by half, but Carlisle had no time for resting on his laurels. Even as he cut the scouting team to pieces, others were advancing toward him, firing as they came. Say ten, eleven men in all, each one intent on killing him to curry favor with Bouchet.

All right, then.

"Come and get it," Carlisle muttered, crouching behind a sturdy tree and waiting for the next pointman to show himself.

It was an awkward feeling, running with her hands behind her back, and twice she almost stumbled, nearly sprawling on her face, but each time Marianne Lacroix was quick enough to catch herself before she fell. Adrenaline was pumping through her veins, her own pulse hammering inside her head, almost as loud as the explosions and staccato gunfire all around.

She didn't really know where she was going. Her first instinct took her back in the direction of the house where she had been confined, but then she caught herself and realized what she was doing. She veered off course and turned right in the direction of the trees. Her sense of direction was normally acute, but fear and disorientation betrayed her now, and she couldn't have said if she was moving to the north, south, east or west. What mattered at the moment was escaping from the open field of fire where men were fighting, dying, bullets buzzing through the air like hungry insects out for blood.

There could be danger in the forest, too, for all she knew: quicksand or snakes, whatever predators were native to the neighborhood. With all the racket from the compound, though, she guessed that any prowling animals in the vicinity would already be fleeing for their lives.

As she was, even now.

She had no way of knowing who had set off the explosives, who was shooting up the compound. Mike Belasko's name came instantly to mind, but how could he have found her, and so quickly, when she herself didn't know where she was? If by some chance it *was* Belasko, then he had to have reinforcements with him from the sound of things. Were they police or federal agents? And if so, where were the flashing lights, the helicopters, bullhorns calling for Bouchet and all his henchmen to surrender?

Where had Bouchet gone?

The question sent a chill of fear through her. She almost stumbled once again, but kept her balance with an effort.

Someone had shot her escorts—she knew that much—but she hadn't waited for Bouchet to act before she took off running for her life. When she glanced back, mere seconds later, he was nowhere to be seen, and the relief she felt, that he wasn't pursuing her, had been enough to blot the *houngan* briefly from her mind.

Now he was back.

She gained the space between two bungalows and paused there for a moment to coordinate her thoughts and catch her breath. The bullets wouldn't find her there, and she could stop to think about what she was doing, what should happen next.

Hands cuffed behind her, there was little she could do in terms of self-defense, and this wasn't the time to see if she could bend her legs and work them through the circle of her arms to put her hands in front. It might be possible, but there was also a fair chance that she would place herself in an untenable position if she tried, and this wasn't the time or place to practice strange contortions, while her enemies were only yards away.

Escape was her priority, and that meant moving deep into the forest—deep enough, at any rate, for her to hide and wait the battle out, see who the victor was before she showed herself again. If Bouchet and his people were defeated, as she hoped they would be, Lacroix could check out the winners from hiding, find out who and what they were. She was prepared to trust herself with any recognizable authorities, but there was still a chance that someone else would make a move against Bouchet—some other drug ring, for example—and she had no wish to wind up as some other desperado's hostage, after she had come this far.

She would have to watch her step. A fall out in darkness could mean injury or worse. If she could only make it to the tree line, find her way inside the brooding shadows, she could relax a little, take her time, make sure she got it right.

But now, right now, she had to move.

The trees were all of fifty feet away, no great expanse of open ground, but guns were going off behind her, and a stray shot could be just as deadly as a bullet aimed to kill. She braced herself, moved out, edged past the corner of the bungalow—

And gasped as someone grabbed her by the hair, and the barrel of a large gun pressed against her neck.

"Now, Marianne," Philippe Bouchet said, "you mustn't leave the party yet."

BOLAN MISSED Bouchet on the fly, a 3-round burst from his carbine that sliced empty air where the *houngan* was standing a split second earlier. Bouchet was running flat out toward the bungalows, head down, arms pumping in time with his knees as he sprinted for safety.

Bolan swung the Colt Commando after him, a portion of his mind with Marianne Lacroix, yet knowing that he had to drop Bouchet before she would be truly safe. He was about to squeeze the trigger, when a gunman from the pack around the bonfire suddenly ran into range, arms waving overhead and calling to his leader in a high-pitched voice. Bouchet glanced over at him, something showing in his ebony face, a glimpse of something dark and dangerous. He saw the runner's shotgun, locking on it with his eyes, and there was sudden hope in place of fear.

On impulse, Bolan swung his rifle slightly to the right and took the runner down, a single round dead center in his back that pitched him forward, sprawling as he fell. Bouchet veered toward him, stooped to grab the shotgun as he passed and reached the nearest bungalow as Bolan found his target, squeezing off another burst. The bullets gouged unpainted wood, missing Bouchet by a foot or less, and he was gone.

Without a moment's hesitation, Bolan set off in pursuit, leaving Carlisle to contain the others while he went after Bouchet. It was for nothing, wiping out the rest, if their *houngan* escaped. The smell of gun smoke clung to the soldier as he ran, boots pounding on the hard-packed earth, along the line of bungalows that formed the compound's northern side.

In front of him, no more than thirty feet from where Bouchet had disappeared, a door flew open, and a tall man, carrying a submachine gun, stepped into the open. He was late arriving at the party, and the stoned expression on his face explained the lapse, as far as Bolan was concerned. Tardy or not, he had arrived, and he was staring straight at Bolan now, hands fidgeting as they began to swing around the SMG.

It was an old Smith & Wesson M-76, long obsolete, but still as deadly as the day it came off the assembly line. The subgun was chambered in 9 mm and held thirty-six rounds in a fully loaded magazine, with a cyclic rate of over 700 rounds per minute in full-auto mode. At that range, even a wasted, half-blind gunner could expect a few square hits, which meant that Bolan had no time to lose.

He hit the groggy shooter with a rising burst of 5.56 mm manglers, stitching him from hip to shoulder with a ragged line of holes that rose across his torso, right to left. The impact spun him like a scarecrow in a hurricane, his SMG lost halfway through the pirouette, before he fell to the ground, without another twitch.

The way was clear, but Bolan kept up his guard, pausing for a heartbeat at the corner where Bouchet had disappeared. He risked a peek between the bungalows, then followed in a rush when he saw no one waiting to surprise him there. A few more yards, and he would see—

The shrill sound of a woman's scream was audible above the sounds of gunfire from behind him. It had come from somewhere off to Bolan's left, beyond the bungalow that hemmed him in on that side. Picking up his pace, he came around the corner in a fighting crouch, the Colt Commando at his shoulder, ready for an aimed shot if he got the chance.

Philippe Bouchet was standing thirty feet away from him, with Marianne Lacroix. The *houngan*'s left hand gripped her hair with force enough to make her head lean toward him, pain etched on her face. In Bouchet's right, the shotgun lifted from his dead disciple pressed against the woman's neck.

"That's far enough, white man."

"Nobody's moving," Bolan replied.

"I'm movin', man, and the woman here is comin' with me."

"I don't think so," Bolan told him, holding steady on his mark.

"You think to stop me?"

"That's the plan."

"Suppose I decide to blow this bitch's head off, then?"

"It wouldn't buy you any time."

"You cared enough to come and fetch her, and now you want to see her dead?"

"I came for you," Bolan said. He refused to look at Lacroix, unwilling to confront the anguish on her face.

"That so? How were you able to find me, white man?"

"One of your believers gave you up. Mason DuBois."

"I'll cut his heart out when I get through with you."

"You missed your chance," Bolan replied.

"So, you did me a favor. I'll do one for you. Give you this bitch, I will, and you let me go."

"Won't work," Bolan said, conscious of the fading combat sounds behind him, gunfire sputtering and dying out, a last explosion from the far end of the compound.

"You're a hard man, whitey."

"It's a hard world," Bolan said.

"So right you are."

The shotgun's muzzle swung away from Marianne Lacroix, toward Bolan, in a short, tight arc. Before Bouchet could squeeze the trigger, the Executioner fired a 3-round burst that closed the gap between them, missing Marianne Lacroix by inches, ripping into Bouchet's face. The *houngan* toppled over backward, dragging her with him, lifeless fingers tangled in her hair. His shotgun fired a wasted charge of buckshot toward the moon.

A heartbeat later, Bolan knelt beside the woman, carefully untangling the dead man's fingers from her hair. She threw her arms around his neck, tears streaming down her face.

"It's all right," Bolan told her. "You're okay now."

Footsteps, closing from behind him, brought the Executioner around, his carbine rising in a stiff one-handed grip. The sights locked on Tom Carlisle's chest and held there for an instant before Bolan let them drop.

"All done back there," the DEA man told him.

"Everybody?"

"Everybody I could see," Carlisle corrected him. "We probably shouldn't hang around to see who crawls out of the woodwork. She all right?"

"She will be," Bolan said. "Let's go."

Haiti is less than half an island, sharing space with the Dominican Republic on a piece of land resembling a lobster claw, four hundred miles in all, from east to west, 150 north to south across the widest point. Haiti is the pincer of the lobster claw, located on the west, perhaps one-third of the island's total land mass, reaching toward Cuba, across the Windward Passage.

Haiti has always been a land where mystery and misery dwelt side by side. Columbus and his Spanish cronies came in search of gold in 1492, and wound up slaughtering the native Arawaks. France was ceded the western part of the jungle isle by Spain in 1697 and turned it into a way station, where African slaves were "seasoned" before they moved on to a lifetime of forced labor on American plantations. The slaves rebelled a century later and, led by dynamic Toussaint L'Ouverture, sent the Frenchmen packing in a brief but grim guerrilla war. One of the side effects of independence was the rise of voodoo to the status of a semi-official religion in Haiti, filling in the gaps where French and Spanish Catholicism had failed to impress a captive people. An outbreak of political violence threatened American economic interests in 1915, prompting an invasion by troops who occupied Haiti until 1934, when a measure of independence was restored with ongoing oversight and financial support from the States. The Duvalier family, embodied in despotic "Papa Doc" and his son, "Baby Doc," ruled Haiti for twenty-eight years, beginning in 1957, with a combination of voodoo and straightforward political terror. New president Jean-Bertrand Aristide was ousted by a military coup in 1991, and the junta's refusal to honor Haiti's new constitution led to savage violence in the streets. American troops returned in 1993, as the spearhead for a UN peacekeeping force, to restore Aristide as president.

Since then, by all accounts, it had been business as usual: corruption and payoffs, disease and starvation, brutality and murder—all with the incessant undertone of magic lurking in the background, mocking Aristide's effort to place his homeland squarely in the twentieth century. A steady flow of Haitian refugees to the United States had caused an immigration crisis for the White House and a law-enforcement crisis nationwide, as some of those who landed in the U.S. continued the criminal activities they had practiced at home, taking full advantage of their political and drug connections in South America and the Caribbean.

All this passed through Mack Bolan's mind as he traveled from New Orleans to Port-au-Prince. He thought about the last time he had gone to Haiti, the unrest and violence he had witnessed—and participated in—as a clandestine prelude to Operation Restore Democracy. With decades of dictatorship behind them, Bolan wondered if the Haitian people even understood democracy, whether the average starving, homeless man in Port-au-Prince would think a ballot box was something he could pawn for pennies, toward a meal of curried fish and rice.

Tom Carlisle had the window seat on Bolan's left. They had debated whether he should tag along, his job and all, but Carlisle had convinced the Executioner with his recital of the contacts he could tap in Haiti, courtesy of DEA, if they ran into any major problems. They were limited, those contacts, but it wouldn't hurt to have a friendly ear or two in Haitian law enforcement when the chips were down.

Corruption made large segments of the national police an adjunct of the drug cartels in Haiti, but, as anywhere, there were loyal officers committed to their oath, still putting in the time, regardless of obstruction by the men upstairs. Some never put their hands out, never sold their badges, even when the kids were going hungry and their wives complained that they could make more money selling farm equipment to the white man.

"Coming up," Carlisle said, and the chiming of a bell inside the cabin validated his assessment of their progress. Overhead, the seat-belt lights came on. The captain's disembodied voice told Bolan they were entering their final approach to Port-au-Prince.

Final approach.

He smiled at that, relieved that he wasn't the superstitious type. The whole thing might have spooked him otherwise. Before they left New Orleans, Marianne Lacroix had given each of them an amulet to wear, but Bolan left his in his suitcase. Tom Carlisle had taken care to hide the leather thong around his neck that morning, but he didn't need to fear that Bolan would have laughed at him.

Whatever got you through.

For Bolan, it was preparation, planning and determination, with a measure of audacity. And he would need all that, in spades, once they landed.

Black magic would be waiting for them on the ground.

And lots of red, red blood.

THE EXECUTIONER'S first target was a *hounfor*—voodoo temple—in the heart of Port-au-Prince, a few blocks west of Rue Capois, near the Museum of Haitian Art. It was the kind of place where tourists were allowed to witness an "authentic voodoo ceremony" for a price, take pictures if they cared to, purchase trinkets in the gift shop and go home believing they had glimpsed the dark heart of an ancient cult. In fact, the rituals displayed for noninitiates were sanitized, a more musical variety than pure black magic, but the tourists always got their money's worth.

It wasn't voodoo, or the prospect of an artsy-fartsy scam, that lured Bolan to the *hounfor,* though. He was attracted by the knowledge that its owner, Eduard Devereaux, was named by Carlisle and the DEA as the godfather of a thriving voodoo-drug cartel with ties to the United States. His front man in New Orleans had been one Philippe Bouchet, and Bolan couldn't shake his feeling that the serpent, although wounded, was a long, long way from dead.

The team at Stony Man had called ahead to fix his meeting with an arms supplier in the Haitian capital, and Bolan paid hard cash for the equipment he required. It was a mixed bag, but with any luck at all, it ought to see them through the next two days or so. If they were still in Haiti after that, it was unlikely military hardware would be any help.

A jacket would have been conspicuous in Haiti's tropic heat, so Bolan packed his stubby MP-5 K submachine gun in a shoulder bag designed for camera gear. His side arm, a Glock 17, was tucked inside his waistband at the back, concealed beneath the loose tail of a baggy cotton shirt. Blue jeans and black athletic shoes completed the ensemble, with a pair of mirrored sunglasses that helped the locals to confuse him with Joe Tourist at a glance.

He passed the *hounfor* on the far side of the street, then crossed and doubled back, passed by again and turned into an alley two doors down. A pride of motley-looking cats trailed Bolan through the alley, far enough to figure out that he wasn't a source of food before they left him to his business. Coming up behind the temple, Bolan tried the back door, found it locked and spent a moment working on the lock before he made his way inside.

So far, so good.

The strong aroma of the place was partly incense, partly barnyard. Bolan guessed that the traditional bloodletting—doves, chickens and goats—was reserved for rituals without a tourist audience. In any case, he didn't need reports from a forensics team to know that fowl and livestock had been quartered there, and recently. There seemed to be no goats or roosters currently in residence, but neither had the human tenants tried to purge their odors from the *hounfor*.

Bolan waited for his pupils to accommodate the murky light, and in the meantime picked up muffled voices emanating from a door halfway along the corridor and to his left. They were male voices, two or three of them, at least, not arguing exactly, but pursuing a discussion that entailed some measure of excitement.

Bolan moved in the direction of the sound, extracting his short stuttergun from cover as he closed the gap. He had the MP-5 K cocked and the safety off as he stepped through the open doorway of a smallish office, covering four Haitians by the time they noticed he was there.

One sat behind a desk, an older man with more meat on his bones, gray traces in his hair. He would have pegged the other three men anywhere from twenty-five to thirty, two of them clean shaved, while the third, on Bolan's far right, had the makings of a scraggly beard and mustache. All three of them were standing, ringed about the desk, and pistols bulged beneath the plain white shirts they wore. All four stared back at Bolan, startled. He couldn't have said if they were more surprised by the machine gun in his hands or by the color of his skin.

"Which one of you speaks English?" Bolan asked.

"We all do," said the man behind the desk. "What do you want?"

"I have a message for your boss."

"My boss?"

"That's Eduard Devereaux. Who wants to be the messenger?"

"What is the message?" Once again, it was the man behind the desk who spoke.

"Just this—he's going out of business in the States and in Haiti. I don't want him griping that he didn't get the word."

"Are you insane?" the man behind the desk inquired.

"I've heard it said."

"You would be wise to leave now."

"Not just yet."

As the bearded man went for his gun, Bolan fired a 3-round burst that slammed him back against a nearby filing cabinet, legs buckling under him as he collapsed. The other two young guns were ducking, dodging, reaching for their hardware, but there was no place for them to hide. He cut them down with short precision bursts, then turned his SMG back toward the man behind the desk.

"Your boss should understand I'm serious," he said. "If he has any other doubts, tell him to ask Philippe Bouchet."

The old man's eyes went wide at that. He nodded and made a point of keeping both hands visible, above the desk-top, so that Bolan wouldn't think he had a weapon stashed below.

"Oh, by the way, you'll want to leave now. Out the front, before you get caught in the fire."

He didn't have to tell the lone survivor twice. The man was up and out of there with an alacrity that was impressive for a man his weight and age. When he was gone, the Executioner dropped an incendiary stick atop his desk and tossed another in the general direction of the *hounfor* proper, at the far end of the corridor. He was outside, back on the main street and a block away, before smoke started curling out the door.

And he had no doubt that the message would get back to Eduard Devereaux, but he wasn't about to trust one lone messenger. The day was young, and he had work to do in Port-au-Prince.

The kind of work that wouldn't wait.

The killing kind.

THE UNEXPECTED always made Jean Grandier nervous. As a member of the Haitian national police force, he had learned to live with sudden, even revolutionary change, but it was one thing trying to adapt, and something else entirely when it came to feeling comfortable with rude surprises. His covert cooperation with the DEA increased the sergeant's usual uneasiness, reminding him each day that many of the officers around him had sold out to drug cartels and smugglers of assorted contraband, from arms to emigrants. He knew some of the sellouts at a glance; with others, even those above him, he could never be completely sure.

There was a risk involved, then, any time he got a call from his connection to the DEA in Port-au-Prince. He didn't think his telephones were tapped at home or work, and there was never much said anyway, except to fix a meeting. Grandier took care to see that no one followed him when he was meeting the American named Sandford, who presumably helped process visa applications to the States from his small office at the U.S. Embassy. They huddled briefly, sometimes passed a sheaf of documents or photographs and wished each other well.

The previous night was different, though. Sandford had called him at home to fix a meeting for that afternoon. A stranger would be showing up in Sandford's place, a black man from America whose name supposedly was Carson. Grandier didn't believe it for a moment, and he didn't care. The meeting was agreed to, but his sleep was ruined for the night. He had to plan ahead, chart out his day, consider what might happen if the meet went wrong.

Carson was waiting for him at the Iron Market, on Rue de Casernés. He wore a flowered tourist shirt and wide-brimmed panama hat over plastic-rimmed sunglasses, and was carrying a red plastic shopping bag in his left hand. The sergeant wore plain clothes and came up on the stranger's blind side, pretending to check out the fruits and vegetables displayed at the nearest produce stall.

"Monsieur Carson?"

The man swiveled to regard him with a frown. "You're Grandier?"

"I'm *Sergeant* Grandier."

"Let's take a walk," the American suggested.

They walked and waited, Tom Carlisle pausing several times to browse among the stalls and check their back-track, glancing all around them, making doubly sure that neither of them had acquired a tail. When he was satisfied, he steered the sergeant off to one side of the market, where the hawkers wouldn't drown out normal speech.

"I'm with DEA," he said at last.

"This much I know."

"We dropped Philippe Bouchet last night, together with a couple dozen of his people in the States."

"Congratulations." Grandier was properly impressed. "When does the trial begin?"

"No trial," the American said. "We had to smoke them."

Grandier blinked at that, uncertain as to how he should respond. When he could find his voice again, he simply asked, "All of them?"

"Looks that way. You've heard of zero tolerance, I guess."

"Not in that context," Grandier replied.

"You had to be there," Carlisle told him. "Anyway, I'm here to do a number on his buddy Devereaux."

"Alone?" The sergeant was amazed.

"Did I say that?"

"No, but—"

"Before we waste a lot of time, you need to know this

is a special operation. No kid gloves, no extradition papers. Do you follow me?''

The sergeant followed him, all right, but didn't like where he was being led. "Who do you work for, really?" he inquired. "The CIA?"

"They don't do drug lords. Anyhow, what's in a name? Shakespeare wrote that, a long time ago. I'd say it still holds true today."

"Why are you telling me all this?" Grandier couldn't help thinking of a setup, someone trying to entrap him, maybe record an untoward comment to use against him later, as the need arose.

"You've got a reputation as an honest cop," Carlisle said, "And you've helped us out before."

"With information only."

"Hey, that's all I'm looking for. Some pointers, here and there. If you'd rather pass, there're no hard feelings. Maybe you should call in sick the next few days."

"What is it that you want to know?" the sergeant asked, still cautious.

"Anything you've got that isn't on our books for Eduard Devereaux. Addresses, known associates, his likes and dislikes, favorite color—anything at all. You never know what comes in handy until you've seen it all."

"And you will use this information to...?"

"Eliminate a problem that has troubled both our countries too long, as it is."

"The man you seek has friends in Port-au-Prince, including some who wear a uniform," Grandier said.

"I'm counting on it. The plan isn't to bother any cops, if they don't bother us. Avoid all contact if we can. As for the politicians, well, who gives a damn what happens to them, right?"

"This is...unusual," Grandier said.

"And then some. Will you help us out or not?"

The sergeant's mind was racing, weighing risks against

the possible rewards. He had seen so much violence in the past twelve years on duty, much of it committed by the government he served, against its citizens, that he had largely grown inured to bloodshed. He still mourned in his heart for guiltless victims, but he had learned to put the hurt away, not let it rule his life. As for the likes of Eduard Devereaux...

"I'll do it. How soon do you need the information?"

"Yesterday. But I could settle for a couple hours down the road."

"We shouldn't come back here," Grandier told him.

"Your call."

"All right, then. Let me think a moment."

He was in it now, surprised to feel a tingling of relief that the decision had been made. It still might ruin his career, or even get him killed, but Grandier had grown adept at self-protection. If worse came to worst, he could flee Port-au-Prince, perhaps flee Haiti. It had crossed his mind a thousand times before, but he had never acted on the urge.

And if it all worked out, then he would have performed a service for his country that, although unrecognized, would help him sleep at night.

He knew the stories about Eduard Devereaux, and it was time for them to end.

"Are you familiar with the Exposition Grounds, on Harry Truman Boulevard?"

"I'll find it."

The sergeant checked his watch. "Two hours, then. Inside the gate."

"I'll see you there."

They separated, and Jean Grandier began to walk back toward his office, mildly startled by the sudden rush of energy he felt inside.

HAITI'S PRIMARY EXPORTS to the world at large are coffee, sugar, cocoa and bananas. It was no surprise, therefore, to learn that Eduard Devereaux was in the coffee business, shipping wholesale to a number of hotel chains in the States and South America. The business turned a tidy profit, and it also gave him ample opportunity to hide his shipments of cocaine in giant sacks of aromatic coffee beans that helped defeat drug-sniffing dogs.

Not that he should have needed any simple tricks, with all that magic on his side, but Bolan knew a wise man always covered all his bets. An item left to chance was the most likely one to blow up in your face and ruin everything.

The coffee warehouse was located on the waterfront. Dusk was approaching rapidly when Bolan got there, scouting from a distance, watching out for sentries that would tell him there was more than coffee presently in-house.

Not that he cared.

Whatever Eduard Devereaux had managed to accumulate in life, by fair means or foul, was subject to forfeiture in Bolan's view, to pay the *houngan*'s debt for crimes against humanity. He wouldn't spare a "simple" coffee business that ostensibly had made Devereaux one of the richest native Haitians on the island. No one ever got around to asking where his first investment capital had come from, how he seemed to beat the competition so consistently. If anyone *had* asked, in Port-au-Prince or in the Haitian countryside, the common answer would have been contained in two short syllables: voodoo.

Fine.

The "magic" hadn't fazed him in New Orleans, and the Executioner had no good reason to believe it would affect him now in Port-au-Prince. He knew the city's dangers well enough from personal experience, and he wasn't concerned about the threat of someone stealing locks of hair, a drop of sweat or clippings from his fingernails to make a voodoo effigy. All's fair in war, and Bolan didn't mind if Devereaux tried using magic on him. He preferred a superstitious enemy, in fact, as one who had more weaknesses, if only psychological, than other men with cooler heads.

Right now, though, Bolan's target was a load of coffee, and whatever else he found inside that warehouse on the waterfront. When he had finished scouting the perimeter, he chose one of at least a dozen tall slits in the chain-link fence that ringed the property and made his way inside. Security seemed minimal, but there was no apparent evidence of vandalism anywhere around the grounds. Perhaps, he thought, the owner's reputation as a man in touch with Baron Samedi and Damballah made the punks and sneak thieves go in search of safer prey.

He climbed a set of concrete stairs and crossed the warehouse loading dock, past giant metal doors with bolts and padlocks, to reach a man-size door down at the other end. This, too, was locked, but after listening for several moments at the door, detecting no sounds from within, he snapped the flimsy lock and let himself inside.

He had the warehouse to himself, from all appearances. If there were any watchmen on the premises, he couldn't find them, and he soon gave up the search. Time was his most important ally at the moment, striking hard and fast at Devereaux before the *houngan* could retaliate, and Bolan couldn't linger overlong on simple torch jobs, when more-difficult procedures lay ahead of him.

Besides the little SMG and extra magazines, his heavy shoulder bag contained two frag grenades, four smallish blocks of plastique, and a fair assortment of incendiary charges. Bolan planted four of those where they would do the most harm and made his way outside once more before the fuses popped.

He didn't have a clue how much the warehouse and the double-roasted coffee would be costing Devereaux in U.S. dollars, and it was beside the point. He had already sent one message to the voodoo lord of Port-au-Prince, and this would be another. Bolan didn't have to sign each one for

Devereaux to know that someone out there wanted him destroyed.

That was enough for now. The rest would come in time.

And time was coming, soon.

The clock was running down in Port-au-Prince, and Bolan wondered if the *houngan* had a premonition of disaster, after what had happened to Philippe Bouchet, or was the crimson magic of the battlefield on *his* side this time?

It could still go either way, but Bolan meant to give it everything he had.

It was the only way he knew to play the game.

10

Claude Manigat had spent the past four decades trying to forget about his roots. A peasant boy from Cap Hatien, five hours north of Port-au-Prince by car, he had been all of six years old the night members of the Tonton Macoutes had come to take his father for a one-way ride. The oldest of four children, he had watched his mother drift from one miserable job to another, finally allowing herself to be "kept" by a planter who used her brutally and mocked her suffering. Manigat wasn't yet twelve the night he crept into the planter's bedroom with a rusty bolo knife and sent him to Damballah. There was nothing he could do, from that point on, but run and keep on running, all the way to Port-au-Prince, where he had joined the ten or fifteen thousand other children living on the street.

He hadn't been the only youthful killer in the gang he joined, but he was easily the smartest of the lot. He kept his eyes wide open, seeking opportunities to bridge the gap between his world and the domain of money, power, style that was so far above him in those early days that it could easily have been a dream. He took odd jobs, stole money when he could and learned to save as much as possible. He started doing odd jobs for a wealthy lawyer in the capital, allowed the older man to think of him as someone who required protection, guidance, leadership. In time, he graduated to a clerking job, went back to school and with his patron's help, himself became a lawyer in due time. He was admitted to the old man's firm, stayed on as others died, retired or moved to the United States. Manigat cultivated friends in government and elsewhere, men of influence who could assist him in his own rise to the top.

One hand washed the other, as they said in the United States, but that didn't imply that either hand was clean.

At fifty-two, Claude Manigat had risen to the rank of special secretary for interior affairs. He had lunch with the president no less than twice a month, and several hundred people counted on him for their daily bread. He did his job effectively, but he was all the more effective in his other occupation, lurking in the shadow of his stately government position.

He had been referred to once—and once only—as the Haitian minister of crime. The young reporter who had coined that phrase was dead now, though his editor and friends believed that he had fled the city with a mistress and a suitcase bulging with embezzled cash. It was a relatively easy case to frame, and he wouldn't be found.

Eduard Devereaux had seen to that.

It was a favor, on Devereaux's part, for the man who made life easier by running interference for him with the national police, ensuring that the brass received their payoffs right on schedule and that they passed some of the money down the chain of command to their ranking subordinates. The street cops did as they were told, and picked up bribes along the way from smaller fish. It was the way things worked in Haiti—in the 1950s, in the 1980s and today.

The more things changed, the more they stayed the same.

Praise be to Damballah.

The thoughts of Devereaux reminded Manigat that it was nearly time for him to meet with his associate again. They kept a schedule, more or less, so that Devereaux would have no reason to suspect that he was being short-changed when it came to information or his share of graft from varied enterprises that were paying Manigat for the privilege of staying in business. Manigat was the front man in those cases, but he relied on Devereaux's muscle if the "clients" resisted, and Devereaux had never let him down. On the other side of the balance sheet, Manigat received monthly payments from Devereaux for his assistance in the coffee business—a legitimate concern that needed government permits to get along—and from assorted other dealings that weren't the stuff of public record.

He was reaching for the telephone, just inches from his elbow on the polished desktop, when a most amazing thing occurred. The telephone exploded, spraying jagged bits of plastic in his face. Manigat recoiled in shock, vaguely aware that something had crashed through his office window, struck the telephone and shattered it.

A stone? Impossible. His fourth-floor office was too far above the street to be at risk from vandals. Turning toward the broken window in his swivel chair, the special secretary saw a hole the size of a fifty-centime coin, with long cracks radiating from it like the strands of a spiderweb. He blinked, was trying to make sense of it, when yet another hole appeared, and something struck the desk beside him with the sharp sound of a hatchet biting into wood.

"My God!"

Manigat knew exactly what was happening. He could hardly make himself believe it, but belief wasn't required. A third shot took out half the window, brought glass raining onto his carpet, but Manigat was on the floor by that time, huddled underneath his desk.

He heard his secretary on the intercom before a bullet knocked the speaker off his desk and dashed it to the floor. She poked her head into the office seconds later, and retreated with a shrill scream when a slug ripped through the wall beside her, inches from her face.

Manigat couldn't have said exactly when the shooting ended. There was noise, then silence, but he waited moments longer, fearing it could be a trick, the sniper waiting for him to reveal himself before he took another shot and finished it. He was resigned to wait beneath his desk all night, if necessary, until help arrived.

And when he made it safely home, the special secretary knew, it would be time to have an urgent talk with Eduard Devereaux. The *houngan* would know what was going on.

He always knew.

JEAN GRANDIER KEPT waiting for the other shoe to drop. It seemed too easy, copying the files on Eduard Devereaux and passing them to the American who called himself Tom Carson. It wasn't the first time Grandier had copied files and given them to agents of the DEA without the knowledge or approval of superiors who would have fired him, at the very least, if they had known what he was doing.

No, the subterfuge was not what troubled him.

There had to be more.

The violence had already started—three men dead, a warehouse and a *hounfor* burned by arsonists, shots fired into the office of a senior secretary with the government. The final incident had startled Grandier, although he knew Claude Manigat was dirty, as the Yanks would say. The vast majority of Haitian officials had their hands out, when it came to bribes, and they weren't at all particular about who paid them, as long as the money kept rolling in. Did Manigat's selection as a target have some special meaning? Was that incident related to the other raids, which had been pointedly directed at the works of Eduard Devereaux?

Grandier was tired of questions and ready to go home, let nature take its course with Devereaux and company, but he couldn't give up that easily. He had a job to do, in spite of the official reticence from his superiors. If he could only do that job by helping the Americans, so be it. He would do what had to be done.

And he would *not* go home. Not yet.

There was no problem with his lingering around the squad room. Haitian officers weren't paid overtime, regardless of the hours they worked, so there was no one breathing down his neck to get him out of there and off the clock. The night shift, coming on, was always glad to find an extra pair of helping hands around the office, anyone to help them with the typing of reports and other chores that came along.

He would be glad to help, as long as it provided him with an excuse to hang around.

The sergeant wondered what was coming next in Carson's war against the Devereaux cartel. How many agents were involved? Would Grandier be asked to help again?

He should be ready, just in case. Not only to assist the Yanks, but to protect himself, as well. It would be bad for him if he was linked to an illegal operation in the capital, where men were killed and someone tried to shoot a special secretary with the government's Interior Department. He wouldn't get off with mere dismissal, in that case. It would mean prison time, and a policeman seldom lasted long in prison—not in Haiti, not in the United States.

It was a simple thing for him to hang around with the investigators working on the several incidents and pick their brains. In fact, they had few clues, no solid evidence at all, beyond some cartridge casings picked up in the ruins of the *hounfor*. That, and a survivor of the first attack who swore that his employees had been executed by a white man. As to why the late "employees" had been armed, the lucky man was clueless. It wasn't his business, not his problem if the others chose to carry guns. Perhaps they felt a need for self-protection, not that it had helped them in the end.

The old man from the *hounfor* couldn't say—or wouldn't say—why he alone was spared in the attack. He made it sound like luck, but Grandier was dubious. A shooter who was good enough to drop three men before they reached their guns was also smart enough to silence any witnesses...unless he needed one of them alive.

But why?

It was a question he could ask Tom Carson, if and when they met again. Meanwhile, he wondered how the fires and shootings were affecting Eduard Devereaux. It was no secret that he owned the *hounfor* and the coffee warehouse that had burned, with several hundred thousand pounds of first-rate coffee beans inside. The property and merchandise would be insured, of course, but this wasn't a simple case of fraud by fire. That wasn't Devereaux's game. He dealt in drugs, extortion, usury, some prostitution on the side. There were suspicions that he also traded slaves, under the guise of labor contracting to large plantations on the island, but the workers didn't file complaints, and their employers were untouchable without sufficient evidence to overcome their weighty bank accounts and guarantee conviction in a court of law.

Perhaps Tom Carson's method *was* the only way. In any case, it ought to shake things up a bit in Port-au-Prince, make Devereaux think twice about his choice of a career.

And when he called upon his gods, then what?

Jean Grandier wouldn't have called himself a superstitious man, but everyone in Haiti knew the voodoo basics and could name at least one neighbor, friend or relative who had been cursed at some point in their lives. Most curses were resolved by settling your differences with an opponent, one way or another. Life went on for most, although survival of a voodoo curse was never absolutely guaranteed. As for himself, the sergeant wasn't a religious man. He worked with facts, hard evidence and human beings.

Still, he hoped that Eduard Devereaux wouldn't discover *his* part in the plot now under way. It would be most unfortunate if that should happen. Most unfortunate indeed.

He concentrated on the conversation of his fellow officers, as much to keep his mind off voodoo curses as for anything that he might learn. It was time to concentrate, and he couldn't afford to let his own imagination carry him away.

He glanced back at his desk, the telephone, and almost hoped that it would ring, that Tom Carson would be on the other end requesting further help. It would be good, Grandier thought, to be involved in taking down the bad guys for a change.

Perhaps, but it was risky, too.

He slouched back in his well-worn chair and settled in to wait.

TOM CARLISLE CHECKED the safety on his Ingram MAC-10 submachine gun, gave the bulky sound suppressor another half twist to make sure it was secure, then slipped the weapon back inside his canvas shoulder bag. It pulled his shoulder down a little, on the right, but that was fine. He liked the machine pistol's reassuring weight, together with the pressure of the Browning automatic pistol tucked inside his belt at his back. The hardware gave him extra confidence and helped him to believe he might come out of this alive.

Carlisle was waiting in the darkness of an alleyway behind a sporting club off Rue Oswald Duran. According to the information he had gleaned from Sergeant Grandier, the place was frequented by members of Eduard Devereaux's drug-dealing cult. Word got around, and locals who might ordinarily have patronized the club went elsewhere. The proprietor made money either way, and he apparently believed that kissing up to one of Haiti's most successful *houngans* would ensure his own success—or his survival, at the very least. A stranger dropping in was either looking for a deal or else he was a crazy tourist with a death wish.

Either way, he could expect to find what he was looking for.

Except this night.

This evening, Death was stopping by the club to make some acquisitions for the other side. Carlisle wasn't a praying man, but he believed in cosmic punishments, rewards, that kind of thing. The scales of justice never really seemed to balance, otherwise. A human monster slaughtered dozens—maybe hundreds, even thousands—and his own death was supposed to even out the score?

No way.

When bad guys bought the farm, Carlisle liked to think about them roasting in the afterlife. It might be superstitious bullshit, but it helped him face the world and keep his act together, knowing—hoping—that some kind of heavy justice would be waiting, even for the ones who got away.

His thoughts came back to the here and now as an explosion rocked the sporting club. The blast was muffled, but he knew it was a hand grenade, Belasko's way of waking up the natives, seizing the initiative and running with it. Carlisle didn't know how many hardmen were inside the club, but he was standing by to deal with any who bailed out and tried to get away. Belasko had instructed him to stay outside and watch the exit, not risk coming in the back and taking friendly fire by accident.

The man didn't have to tell him twice.

He drew the Ingram from his shoulder bag and waited, covering the door, ten feet way. He heard all kinds of firing in there and had an urge to scrap his orders, have a little look inside, regardless. He was smooth enough to keep his head down, watch his ass. Of course, there *was* a risk that in the heat of battle, not expecting friendly faces on the wrong side of the firing line, all black men might begin to look alike.

Carlisle cautioned himself to stay put and do his job.

That almost made him laugh out loud. This gig was so

far from his job that Carlisle would be looking at a major prison sentence if it ever got back to the brass. They could be looking for him even now, for all he knew, after the blowout on the gulf. He had reported briefly to his handler, said that he was handling some leads, a few loose ends. He might be out of touch for several days, no sweat. But if they really started looking into it, his ass was grass.

The door flew open, right in front of him, and three men piled out in a rush. The first two carried pistols in their hands, and number three was reaching for some kind of weapon underneath his baggy shirt. But they were plainly scared to death, with no intent of going back inside the club to fight it out.

The pointman got a glimpse of Carlisle as the Ingram opened up and swept the three of them with hot 9 mm rounds. None of them had a chance to fire before the silenced bullets ripped into their flesh and took them down, all dumped together in a thrashing, dying heap.

Too easy?

Carlisle braced himself and watched the door, tense now, aware of sudden, deathly silence in the club. A smell of gun smoke reached his nostrils, whether from his own piece or the open doorway, he couldn't say with any certainty. Nor, at the moment, did he give a damn.

He heard someone approaching from the inside of the club, slow footsteps, cautious, drawing closer to the threshold.

''Tom?''

It was Belasko's voice. He let himself relax.

''It's clear.''

The tall man stepped outside, his machine pistol disappearing back inside the matching shoulder bag he carried.

''I left something for the graveyard shift. We should go.''

Bolan didn't have to ask him twice.

They were a block away, and almost to their car, when

the explosion came. It wasn't muffled this time, and it was no simple hand grenade.

"Remodeling?" he asked.

"Urban renewal," Bolan said with a smile.

"Oh, yeah. I heard of that."

"We've still got lots to do."

"Okay," Carlisle replied, sliding in behind the wheel. "Let's get it done."

PAUL THIBIDEUX WAS furious. He hated it when circumstances ran away from him, confounded him and added trouble to his life. As a lieutenant in the national police, he had enough responsibilities just keeping track of thieves and dissidents, the independent gangsters who believed they could survive without protection from the law, without contributing their fair share to the Thibideux retirement fund. The last thing he or anybody needed was a shooting war in Port-au-Prince.

He tried to think of someone in the capital who was fool enough to start a war with Eduard Devereaux. On top of that, they had a failed attempt to kill Claude Manigat, a botched assassination that might or might not be related to the other violent incidents. It wasn't Thibideux's responsibility to solve the crimes himself alone, but he was heading up the detail, and he knew that Devereaux would be expecting something extra for his money. Thibideux earned twice as much from Devereaux's syndicate as from his normal salary, but it wasn't a gift. He had to work for every centime of that money, making sure investigations came to nothing, warning his detectives off a case if it appeared that his associates' interests would be jeopardized.

This was a new one, though. It was the first time anyone had dared to tackle Devereaux head-on that the lieutenant could remember. It was certainly the first time any rash competitor had scored so many points against the *houngan* on his own home turf. The losses had been mounting—

money, men and property—with no end yet in sight. Devereaux would almost certainly be making magic now, to hex his faceless enemies, but that didn't excuse the others on his payroll from performing as he would expect.

Across the squad room, Thibideux saw Jean Grandier still at his desk, no great surprise, considering the circumstances. Crime waves were a rare phenomenon in Port-au-Prince, where most of the arrests were minor, the arrestees poor, their ultimate indictment and conviction a foregone conclusion. Haitian police didn't stalk major crime lords, crooked politicians or successful businessmen who sometimes bent the law. There were traditions to uphold, and one of those was taking what you could, when it became available, to help yourself.

Still, there were some, like Grandier, who never felt at ease with payoffs. Few of them objected openly—it was the swiftest ticket to dismissal or an ugly "accident"—but you could never really trust the righteous ones. It felt like they were always watching, taking notes and looking for a chance to undermine the hard work of a lifetime. Thibideux did everything within his power to keep them occupied with busywork, expose them periodically to new temptation, hoping one of them would slip and soil himself, become a real part of the team, but there was only so much he could do.

He wondered what would happen if a man like Grandier found out who was responsible for the attacks on Eduard Devereaux. Would he report it from a sense of duty, or sit back and watch the fun, believing it could make a difference in the cosmic scheme of things?

He would bear watching, that one, while the heat was on. But first, Paul Thibideux had orders to report to his superior. For that, he had to leave the station. He was scheduled for a meeting with his *real* boss.

When the *houngan* called, it wasn't wise to hesitate.

11

Eduard Devereaux despised confusion. His whole life had been a struggle to bring order out of chaos, on the earthly plane and in the worlds beyond. He had adopted voodoo and rejected Christianity long years ago, because the former system offered steps a man could take to shape his destiny, gain wealth and fame, destroy his adversaries, while the latter told its supplicants to spend a lifetime begging on their knees.

No, thank you.

Devereaux had always been a man of action, who had fought his way up from the streets of Port-au-Prince to rule a billion-dollar empire. Voodoo helped, not only by intimidating those less educated and sophisticated than himself, but by instilling him with confidence that money couldn't buy. His magic didn't *always* work, of course—sometimes he had to help it out with muscle on the streets—but when it did, he felt the power surging through him in a rush akin to sex, and yet more powerful.

The master *houngan* was a true believer, all the way.

But voodoo couldn't seem to help him with his present difficulty. Someone had arrived to challenge him in Port-au-Prince. That challenge came hot on the heels of the disaster in Louisiana, with Philippe Bouchet. The master *houngan* didn't miss Bouchet, per se, but they had built a thriving operation in New Orleans, spreading out across the South, and most of it was gone now, only scattered dealers and a few young soldiers left. He would be forced to start from scratch there, even if he borrowed people from his colony in southern Florida, and in the meantime, various competitors would be at work among his customers, seducing them away in droves.

Still, there was nothing he could do about it at the moment, with his own house threatened by a raging fire. He had to save himself, his base of operations, prior to branching out and fighting on the fringes of his empire. And, he thought, the real solution might be here in Port-au-Prince. If he could only trace his daring enemies and wipe them out, there was at least a fair chance that his other problems would evaporate.

So, he had summoned the lieutenant for a briefing on official progress, and the master *houngan* didn't like what he was hearing. Facing him across the massive desk, Paul Thibideux looked small and ineffectual, a shrunken vestige of the man whose name was used by many peasants to control their children.

"You have nothing for me, then?" Devereaux asked, the hard edge of his voice razor sharp.

"We're working on it," the lieutenant said, eyes downcast, shifting in his chair.

"You're working on it?"

"Yes, sir."

"What of Manigat?" Devereaux asked.

"We have no suspects yet, but it is known that he has enemies. Subversives, radicals...we're checking several groups for possible connections—"

The lieutenant lost his voice and train of thought as Devereaux slammed his fist down on the desktop with force enough to jolt a sharp ping from his telephone.

"You're wasting time," the master *houngan* said. "I've lost more than a dozen men, and several million dollars' worth of property. A ranking member of the government was almost murdered in his office. Does a link between these various events suggest itself to you?''

"I'm checking that," Thibideux said. "My men—"

"Know less now than they did eight hours ago. Must I do everything myself?''

Thibideux glanced at the effigy of Baron Samedi standing in the corner of the office, behind Devereaux and to his left. The officer was blinking rapidly; he had to stop and clear his throat before he spoke.

"Of course, if you could help us—"

"*Help* you? Do your job, is what you mean to say. It's not enough I double your pathetic salary each month and help you cover up your various mistakes. Do you recall the girl in Pétion-Ville, lieutenant?''

"Yes." The word sounded like a strangled whisper from the grave.

"Now I must also do your job, protect myself against attackers no one can identify. I don't think I've received my money's worth, do you?''

"No, sir."

"So, we agree on something. Would you like the payments to continue, Paul, or shall I help you find another line of work? Cane cutters are in short supply, I'm told.''

There was no disguising the fear in the lieutenant's eyes. He knew exactly what the master *houngan* meant. When Devereaux sent someone to the fields, he sent a *zombi* who wouldn't return.

"I want my job," the terrified lieutenant said.

"Then do your job! Stop hiding in the station house and get out on the street. Ask questions for yourself, and don't expect your men to think of everything. They're brainless, most of them."

"Yes, sir."

"You have a reputation to protect, if nothing else," Devereaux said. "Remember who you are—or who you *were*, at least—and do your job!''

"I will."

"Then, go. And keep in touch, Paul. I'll be waiting."

Thibideux got out of there as quickly as he could, so hasty that he almost tripped and fell. It would have been hilarious in other circumstances, but the master *houngan* saw no humor in the present situation. He was fighting for his reputation, at the moment, with an enemy he couldn't identify.

If it kept up, he would be fighting for his life.

"SO FAR, SO GOOD," Tom Carlisle said as they sat sipping coffee in the dark.

"It could be better," Bolan told him.

"Oh?"

"We need to rock this town so hard the cops and papers can't pretend they never heard of Eduard Devereaux."

"Or we could take him out right now," Carlisle suggested, still surprised at just how easily the notion came to mind. It felt almost as if his years of working for the DEA, of fighting for the good guys, had evaporated like a layer of fog before the rising sun.

"Not yet," Bolan replied. "We drop him now, somebody else steps in to take his place, and the machine keeps rolling, like before. We need to spike the engine, put a little sugar in the gas tank, maybe cut the tires before we take the driver down."

"Hey, it was just a thought."

"What's up with your connection at the local cop house, Tom?"

"Don't know. We've been busy since he passed the information off, you know? Supposedly he's hanging out and keeping track of any buzz around the shop. He can't call me, of course. I'd have to check it out."

"You might as well," Bolan said, "before it gets too late."

"You want another meet?"

"Whatever works for you. I won't be there."

"Hey, you tryin' to blow me off?"

"Not even close. We've got a ton of work to do. No point in two men standing still, when one can keep the ball in play."

"Because I don't like bein' taken for granted you know?"

"I hear you."

"I'll make the call. You want this car?"

Bolan shook his head. "Keep it. I'll take the Ford. Just drop me off."

They had acquired two rental cars on reaching Port-au-Prince—in case the two of them got separated, was the way Belasko phrased it, but Carlisle knew that he meant in case one of them bit the dust.

And it could happen, any time. The years of undercover work had taught him there were always new, intriguing ways to die on any job. The gloves were off, this time, since he was far beyond the bounds of his established jurisdiction, way to hell and gone past any vestige of legitimate authority. If Devereaux got lucky, killed him now, the odds were excellent that any Haitian court would call it self-defense and let him walk.

Okay.

He knew the rules, but that didn't mean he was bailing out. He had no family at home—no *home,* to speak of— no one who would miss him if he blew it and the crazy voodoo island swallowed him alive. There would be inquiries if he didn't go back, but that was someone else's problem. Once you were dead, there was nothing anyone could do to help or punish you. All bets were off.

He twisted the ignition key and put the rental car in motion, aiming for the nearest street that would return him to the district where the Ford was stashed. Ten minutes, tops, unless they hit an unexpected traffic jam.

Fat chance.

He was already thinking through the conversation he would have with Grandier, how he would ask the man to meet him one more time. It was a risk, he realized, but so was everything in life. The sergeant didn't seem to mind, and maybe he could help them move the game along.

CLAUDE MANIGAT DETESTED hiding. It didn't befit a man of his position in society to run and hide from peasants, like the lowest kind of coward, but what choices did he have? If there were people desperate enough to try to kill him in his office, what would stop them from attacking him at home, or on the public street? He was afraid, no doubt about it, but his wounded dignity still pained him all the same.

The hideout was a small apartment in the northern part of Port-au-Prince. He kept the place for the occasional liaisons with young women who prevented him from feeling ancient, out of touch with life. Manigat's wife would never understand his needs, so he had kept the place a secret all these years. He had no steady mistress—that was asking for betrayal and embarrassment—but he still used the flat four days a month, on average, with prostitutes. This evening, when he found that he couldn't prevent reports of the attack from circulating, he had called his wife and told her he was going out of town for several days, on orders from his minister.

That ought to keep her quiet for a week at least.

And by that time, he hoped, someone—police or otherwise—should have identified and punished those responsible for the assault.

Meanwhile, he had no choice but to protect himself as best he could...and wait.

There was a pistol on the coffee table, and he had two bodyguards on watch, across the street. There was no rear approach to the apartment—no escape out back, for that matter—and he refused to have the gunmen come upstairs, where they would crowd him out of house and home. It was enough that he had to hide this way, and that their presence would deny him any vestige of companionship while he was suffering in exile. Let them sit in the car and sweat until the next shift came and gave them some relief.

It suddenly occurred to him that they might fall asleep and leave him helpless, but he couldn't bring himself to go downstairs, across the street, to check on them. It was the final straw. He hadn't worked this hard and come this far to risk his own life in the darkness, checking on the hired help like a foreman in some miserable sweatshop.

They would stay awake because they knew their jobs—indeed, their very lives—depended on protecting him from harm. The guards knew who he was and who his friends were, what would happen to them if they failed. Dismissal was the least of it, the very smallest of their problems if they let him die.

That train of thought led Manigat back to the brooding anger he had come to feel for Eduard Devereaux. It seemed to him that the attack on his office had to be linked somehow to the explosive string of incidents in Port-au-Prince that had been targeting Devereaux's syndicate since midafternoon. What other explanation could there be? Coincidence? The very thought was laughable.

So it was Devereaux's fault, however indirectly, and he seemed unable to control the situation. When Manigat reached him on the telephone, Devereaux had spoken to him as if Manigat were someone's simple-minded child. It was infuriating, and the politician had to stop himself from screaming insults through the telephone at Devereaux, whose protection, and the fear his name invoked, might well turn out to be Manigat's last line of defense.

Except for one small thing: the man or men responsible for shooting up his office, and for killing Devereaux's men around the city, burning down his property, didn't behave as if they were afraid. Quite to the contrary, in fact. They were inviting Devereaux to retaliate, if he could only find out who they were.

And that, so far, had been the rub.

It seemed incredible that the police, with all their spies, and Devereaux, with all his goons, couldn't identify the men responsible for these attacks. It almost made him wish the military junta could return to power—long enough, at least, to use their little tricks and find out what was happening. No one had harbored any secrets from the government in those days, or when the Duvaliers were in the presidential palace. It was sad but true that a democracy had certain built-in weaknesses, such as a peasant's right to privacy. That right, in turn, allowed the lower classes to concoct fantastic schemes and plot against their betters, squatting in their filthy hovels, wishing they could steal the treasures decent men had worked so long and hard to gain.

Bemoaning change wouldn't save Manigat from those who stalked him, though. The faceless men who clearly ranked him with the likes of Eduard Devereaux might stop at nothing. They had tried to kill him once already, foiled by haste or shoddy marksmanship. Manigat knew he should be thankful that he was alive, and part of him rejoiced at his escape from death, but he couldn't relax while he knew there were strangers out there, in the city, hunting him as if he were some kind of animal.

Perhaps they would get tired of tracking him and concentrate on Devereaux. It was a hope that he could cling to, but it didn't put his mind at ease. He took the pistol from the coffee table, turned it over in his hands and wished that he had taken time to learn its proper use. He knew enough to cock it, aim and pull the trigger, but there was a world of difference, Manigat supposed, between the thought of it and firing bullets at another human being. Part of it was nerve, and he would force himself to fire, if it came down to that, but he was frightened that his trembling hands would make it all a wasted effort.

He would do what he had to do, he told himself, but took no comfort in the thought. The men who fired into his office might have missed, but they were still competent with weapons, with the thought of killing, whereas he had spent a lifetime trying to unlearn the brutal lessons of the streets.

Now Manigat could only wonder if he might have done the job too well. His life was on the line, and he had major doubts about his own ability to help himself.

He would rely upon the guards outside, then, and on Devereaux, to find their common enemies and wipe them out.

If even one of them survived, Claude Manigat was fairly certain he would never rest in peace again.

"WE CAN'T KEEP meeting like this."

Grandier had spent a quarter of an hour rehearsing that line, making sure he had the proper tone of voice, and it surprised him when the man he knew as Tom Carson laughed.

"Hey, that's a good one. I didn't know you had a sense of humor."

"What?"

"Forget it. Listen, I need an update on what's shakin' at the cop shop."

"Shaking?" Grandier was on the verge of being hopelessly confused.

"What's happening with the investigation?" Carlisle asked him, sounding out the final word by syllables, as if he were communicating with an idiot.

The sergeant frowned and said, "I'm not a child."

"Hey, man, I'm on a schedule here, you know? Things are gettin' tight. I've got to get a move on here."

"Of course. Lieutenant Thibideux has been assigned to the investigation, as coordinator of a special task force. They have no real evidence so far, except for the description of a white man at the *hounfor* that was burned. A poor description, I would say. The witness was...upset.''

''I wouldn't be surprised. Is anybody going after Devereaux?''

''You can't be serious.''

''Forget I asked that, okay? How about that secretary, what's his name?''

''Claude Manigat.''

''Yeah, that's the guy. He hidin' out, or what?''

The sergeant shrugged. ''I've heard nothing about him since the shooting.''

''Yeah, okay. Have the police got any place staked out? You know, protected?''

''Not that I've heard. It would be like admitting they had known where Devereaux conducted business all along, you understand?''

''It's solid, man. So, nothin' on that list you gave me has official cover, as of now?''

''Nothing official, no. There are response teams standing by.''

''Okay, I hear you. Listen, is it safe for me to call you at the shop—your office—if I need to ask you something?''

Grandier considered that, the possibility that someone would be listening when he picked up the telephone, and finally discounted it. He couldn't picture anyone in the department where he worked as being that well organized.

''It should be safe,'' he said at last.

''Okay. I'll try to keep in touch. You got a story, if somebody asks you where you were?''

''I'll think of something,'' Grandier replied.

''All right, then. Watch your ass, man.''

''Watch *your* ass.''

''I'm keeping one eye on it all the time.''

The sergeant walked back to his car without a backward glance at Carlisle, slid behind the wheel and twisted the ignition key. He checked his rearview mirror, pulling out, and saw the road was clear. He didn't check again for several blocks, and thereby missed the car that fell into its place behind him, running without lights until they reached a major thoroughfare and other traffic came between them, running interference.

Sergeant Grandier felt safe.

And he couldn't have been more wrong.

12

Haiti does not produce cocaine in any quantity, although the climate and geography that make coffee a leading export for the island nation are as favorable to production of the coca leaf as are the mountains of Colombia. In fact, the island's modest size, its generations of involvement with—if not outright domination by—America and the facility with which an island can be quarantined have all prevented Haiti from aspiring to the status of a major drug-producing nation.

It is a different story, though, when Haiti's service as an international transshipment station is considered. Just as the Bahamas and Jamaica have become way stations for cocaine en route to the United States from South America, so Haiti serves the shippers and receivers as a kind of middle ground, where bargains can be made and orders placed, with a certain percentage down and full payment on delivery. There is a difference in Haiti, though, where the pervasive U.S. influence and decades of despotic rule have made it difficult, if not impossible, for the Colombian cartels to put their own men in the driver's seat. In Haiti, drugs are purchased by the native godfathers at wholesale prices and repackaged prior to shipment and resale in the United States.

That knowledge brought Mack Bolan to the weathered, rusting hulk of what had once been a dilapidated coffee mill a half mile south of Port-au-Prince. The place was dark when he arrived, with a deserted look, but Bolan knew that it was occupied and doing business seven days a week. Instead of grinding coffee beans, the place now bagged and tagged cocaine.

And it was owned by Eduard Devereaux.

He checked the ground-floor windows, but rusty plates of metal had been welded over them like shutters, making it impossible for prying eyes to see inside. The doors were covered by alarms, and Bolan didn't want the soldiers on his back this soon. Instead, he found the long-abandoned fire escape and tested it to see if it would hold his weight.

It did.

Above the second floor, the owners had grown lazy, painting over windows rather than applying metal plates. Perhaps their minds rebelled at being welded up inside a rusting metal tomb, or maybe they were cheap, just lackeys working in a billion-dollar racket who had saved the boss a hundred bucks on paint.

Go figure.

Bolan took his time on the window, hoping the sound wouldn't carry too far as he cut a fist-sized hole beside the latch and reached in to unlock it. Spiderwebs were tangled on his fingers when he got the job done, and Bolan wiped the hand against his jeans. There were no guards upstairs apparently, and no alarms. When they were laying out defenses for the place, it had to have slipped their minds that anyone could enter from above the working level and climb down.

It made things that much easier, knowing he wasn't dealing with a troop of rocket scientists.

He let himself inside and closed the window, making sure no errant draft betrayed him prematurely. He was on an empty floor that had apparently been used for storage in the old days; support pillars were situated every twenty feet or so, with thick layers of grit and dust beneath his feet. There were no recent tracks of human beings, but the rats were out in force, their scuttling trails reminding him of crab tracks on a beach.

He found the stairs and started down, the Uzi braced against his hip and covering each new turn in the stairwell as it was revealed to him. He found another vacant floor on two, although a few stray wooden crates were stacked up near the stairs. He could hear voices down below, conversing in patois. He didn't understand a word of it, and didn't care. The numbers mattered, not what anyone downstairs had on his mind.

He palmed a frag grenade and pulled the safety pin, but didn't drop it, doing everything he could to minimize the noise of his approach. He left it looped around his little finger, like a friendship ring, and edged his way a little farther down the stairs until he had a clear view of the working area.

It was set up like an assembly line, with kilo bricks of pure Colombian cocaine at one end of a waist-high table, flunkies lined up on both sides with kitchen scales, assorted scoops and spoons and stacks of empty plastic bags. They weighed and measured to the gram before they sealed a bag and passed it to the far end of the table, where an old man with his shirt off double-checked the weight of every bag before he put it in a box that sat beside him on the floor. Four gunners had the corners of the room staked out. Like Bolan, everyone on the assembly line wore a mask to keep from breathing in stray particles of coke.

He counted thirteen men, but only four of them were armed, as far as he could tell. With mask and goggles snug in place and the time run down, he pitched the frag grenade, a gentle underhand that dropped it in the middle of the table, bouncing once before it wobbled to a halt. The drones were gaping at it when it blew, scattering their bodies, throwing up a crystal cloud that fogged the room.

The four young gunners were smart enough to hold off firing in the absence of a target, knowing they could hit each other if they started firing blind. The Executioner had no such problem, and his SMG was hammering the nearest corner as he charged downstairs. Rewarded with a cry of pain, he swung around to face the other gunman who was closest to him, saw a shadow-shape advancing through the fog and cut it down.

The other two were firing now, and Bolan hit the floor. Converging streams of fire crossed overhead, and he could hear the bullets whining as they ricocheted off walls, the floor, the ceiling. Out of nowhere, he saw a figure lurching toward him, one leg dragging, and he swung his SMG in that direction, but the voodoo gunners beat him to it, taking down their own man in a storm of bullets.

Bolan wriggled toward the long steel table, which had buckled, flopping over on its side when the grenade went off. He felt the grains of powder settling on his face and hands, knew he would need a shower when he finished this job.

When he was in position, Bolan risked a peek above the twisted cover of the table and saw the cloud of coke settling, while his two adversaries edged closer to each other, looking for a target in the wreckage of the lab. The gunner on his left said something in patois, a question, and his partner shook his head. A few more steps, and they were rubbing shoulders, standing almost back-to-back and checking out the mess, both wondering what had happened to their enemy.

Bolan gave them several more seconds to think about it, getting ready for the move that would be all or nothing. With his two opponents both packing automatic weapons, he would have to get it right the first time. There would be no second chance.

The Executioner burst from cover with the Uzi spitting death, pitched over to his left and made it through a shoulder roll, still firing all the way. Across the smoky room, his targets were reacting, pivoting to track the unexpected target with their SMGs, but they were out of time. A stream of parabellum shockers slammed them both against the wall, and they left crimson skid marks as they slithered to the floor. He left them slumped together, one's head resting on the other's shoulder, weapons lying useless on the floor beside their outstretched legs.

It took five minutes longer to set up the plastic charges and synchronize detonators. Bolan used the door on his way out, and he was running by the time the place went up, a thunderclap behind him, reaching out to help him with a mighty shove between the shoulder blades.

There had been several hundred kilos of cocaine inside the factory, but Bolan didn't even try to calculate the loss. A million dollars here, a million there—it hardly mattered in the long run. Eduard Devereaux would feel the heat regardless of the price, and he would go ballistic when he heard the news.

It was reward enough for now.

PAUL THIBIDEUX approached the desk were Jean Grandier was typing a report in triplicate. He had been watching Grandier for half an hour, wondering if he could do what had to be done, before he finally decided there was no alternative.

The man was obviously up to something, sneaking out for secret meetings with a stranger, then returning to the station house as if nothing had happened. Thibideux was glad that he had planned ahead, detailed a man to keep an eye on Grandier. It was a curious assignment, granted, but the officer he chose was one who took his share of money on the side, from Eduard Devereaux and others. When he heard that something wasn't right with Grandier, he hadn't hesitated to participate in the surveillance. Now that it was done, the lieutenant had no doubt that the man would keep his mouth shut.

If he tried to talk, well, there was no rule that *two* policemen couldn't have fatal accidents.

It was a bitter thing for Thibideux to order the elimination of another cop, but he was crystal clear on the necessity of rapid action. Grandier's clandestine meetings might have no link to the recent raids in Port-au-Prince, but the coincidence was startling, to say the least. First, Grandier had volunteered to work on when his shift was over, helping out around the office while the task force looked for any clues to the identity of those responsible for the attacks. Then he sneaked out—once, that they knew of—for a hasty meeting with a man who wasn't part of the police force. Thibideux would have the stranger's photo in another thirty minutes, once the prints came back, and he would pass them on to Devereaux, perhaps hold back a copy for himself.

He had already called ahead; the plans were made. Now all he had to do was send the sergeant on his way, sit back and wait for news of the impending tragedy. Of course, he wouldn't be within a mile of the location, and there would be nothing to connect him with the crime.

There never was.

Grandier glanced up at Thibideux and missed a keystroke, cursed, backspaced, typed over the mistaken letter. Using an eraser with the carbon paper made a mess that needed an interpreter to figure out.

"You're busy?" the lieutenant asked.

"I'm typing a report for Bertrand, from his notes," Grandier replied. "He had to take another call."

"The paperwork can wait," Thibideux said. "I have a job for you."

"Oh, yes?" The sergeant stopped typing, half turned in his chair, his eyes fixed on the lieutenant's face.

"We have a witness to the warehouse fire. I think so, anyway. A passerby. Somebody needs to visit him. The buses aren't running now, and he can't get here by himself.''

''You want him brought back here?'' Grandier asked.

''Or you could question him at home. I trust your judgment.''

''Ah.''

The corners of the sergeant's mouth turned down in a subtle frown, and Thibideux was worried that he might have gone too far. He didn't get along that well with Grandier—the two of them were never friends—and Thibideux was well aware of how the sergeant felt about those officers who took a little something extra on the side. Self-righteous to a fault, this one was, but his one redeeming virtue was efficiency. When Grandier was on a job, the job got done.

''You'll help us, then?'' Thibideux asked, not pushing it.

''Of course. I need a name and the address.''

''Right here.''

He passed a slip of paper to the sergeant's outstretched hand. The phony name and the real address had both been typed, and Thibideux took care to smear his fingerprints as he released the only corner of the paper he had touched. Not that the paper would be found, if things went well, but you could never be too cautious.

''I'll go now,'' Grandier said, already on his feet and circling around the desk.

''All right, then. See you soon.''

But not alive, he thought. The next time Thibideux saw Grandier, the sergeant would be in a body bag.

He didn't want to think about the ambush, what was coming, but he couldn't help himself. Devereaux hadn't discussed the details, naturally, but he was interested in having words with Grandier in case the sergeant knew who was responsible for the attacks. He would be killed in either case, a form of cheap insurance, but it would be best if he could help the cause before he died.

A dull ache started to throb behind Thibideux's left eye. He recognized a tension headache coming on, and walked back to his tiny office, where he had painkillers and a whiskey bottle in his desk. The whiskey violated regulations, but it was the least of his accumulated problems at the moment. He would take his chances, try to wash the pain away and focus on survival in a situation that had quickly gone from bad to worse.

It had begun with Eduard Devereaux in trouble, which was only natural, considering his choice of occupations. Then someone had tried to kill Claude Manigat, and that was most unusual. Now Thibideux had been alerted to a traitor in his own backyard, compelled to take stern measures to protect himself, and he could only wonder if there might be more spies in the squad room, someone watching *him*, while he was looking out for number one.

If so, then it was probably too late for him to save himself, but he would have to try. It wasn't in his nature to lie down and wait for grief to overtake him. He would fight until the bitter end, and when the end came, he would face it on his own terms, like a man.

Or maybe he would find an opportunity to simply disappear.

Escape was looking better all the time.

JEAN GRANDIER DROVE slowly, searching for the address that the lieutenant had given to him. He had failed to recognize the name—Gaston Duprée—but that was no surprise. There were at least three-quarters of a million people living in the Haitian capital, and no good reason why a national policeman should know a common workman who was passing by a warehouse when the place went up in flames.

He *had* to be a common man, based on his address, in the southwest quarter of the city. It wasn't a slum, by any means, but the families who lived there had been crowded into two- and three-room flats, with barely room enough to turn around. Most shared a bathroom with their neighbors, and their garbage wound up in the streets and alleyways as often as it reached the nearest container. Stray cats prowled the darkness, hunting mice and rats, while thin, mean-tempered dogs included felines on their menu. They also threatened smaller children now and then, but no one much complained.

In Port-au-Prince, it was a way of life.

He found the address, drove past and made a U-turn in the middle of the street. Most of the windows in the complex were already dark. The workday started early, for those lucky enough to have jobs, and working men needed their sleep. He sat there for a moment, with the engine idling, and he wondered what was going on behind those shabby stucco walls. How many children dreamed of things that only children understood? How many lay awake and listened to their parents arguing, perhaps to sounds of violence from adjoining rooms?

So many secrets were there, the sergeant thought, and only one of them was meant for him.

I trust your judgment. The lieutenant's words were strange enough. It struck Grandier as even more peculiar that Thibideux wouldn't have the witness look at photographs in an attempt to match their suspect with a name.

Unless...what?

Something nagged at the back of Grandier's mind, warning him to slow down, take his time. He was about to kill the engine, step out of the car, when something caught his eye across the street. Was it a spark? And what did that mean if it was?

He stared hard, waiting, and he saw the wink of crimson light a second time. Someone was smoking, over there, the glowing ember of a cigarette a beacon in the night. Why should that be suspicious?

Glancing to his right, the same side of the street where

he was parked, the sergeant saw a subtle movement in the shadows of an alley mouth, some twenty feet in front of him. It was too large to be a cat or dog, so that meant it had to be a human being. At least one, then, on each side of the street.

A trap?

The sergeant felt his stomach churning. Thibideux had sent him on this call. If it turned out to be an ambush, that could only mean that the lieutenant was involved. A sudden rage seized Grandier, but he restrained himself, intent on finding out exactly what was happening before he thought of getting even.

He would have to be alive to get revenge.

He reached inside his lightweight jacket and removed his pistol, thumbing off the safety as he watched the darkened street. If he didn't move soon, the watchers would assume that there was something wrong, and they would have to come for him...unless the ambush was a figment of his own imagination.

On the other hand, he was at liberty to simply drive away and see what happened next. If someone followed him or tried to stop him, then he knew there could be no mistake.

And Thibideux would pay for his duplicity.

The sergeant placed his pistol in his lap, released the parking brake as quietly as possible and put his car in gear. The lights were off, but they would see him when he started rolling, any second...now!

He stood on the accelerator and steered with one hand while the other gripped his weapon. Grandier was ready when the muzzle-flashes bloomed on either side of him, and bullets started hammering his car. A few more seconds, and—

A hulking garbage truck pulled out in front of him to block the street. He slammed on the brakes, ducked as bullets cracked the windshield of his car. He downshifted into reverse and put more weight on the accelerator, smoking rubber as he left the garbage truck behind. He cranked the steering wheel around, prepared to make another screeching turn, but something suddenly went very, very wrong.

It took a moment more for Grandier to realize that one of his front tires was flat. A bullet had to have found it in the darkness, luck or steady marksmanship betraying him. He lost acceleration, felt the rim bite into asphalt, trailing sparks. The wheel jerked in his hand, as if the car were trying to rebel against its driver. Grandier fought hard to hold it straight, but he could feel the rear end drifting to his right, in the direction of the curb.

He hit a street sign, sheared it off ten inches from the ground and bounced across the curb. Too late, he saw the corner of another building loom behind him, then he struck it with a sound of metal snapping under stress. His engine flooded, stalled and died.

Grandier was twisting the ignition key in vain, and cursing to himself, when bullets started peppering the car once more. He ducked his head below the level of the dashboard, tried the engine one more time and heard the sound of bullets ripping through his grille into the radiator.

It was finished.

If he sat still, he would surely die.

The sergeant took a firm grip on his pistol and used its butt to crush the dome light. That done, he reached across the seat and crawled out on the far side of the car. The firing picked up instantly, no less than half a dozen guns, with several flanking him on each side of the street.

Where could he go? They would be waiting for him when he made his move. He thought of the lieutenant, waiting back at headquarters, and fantasized of coming up behind him with a baseball bat to crush his skull.

The smell of gasoline cut through his fleeting reverie, and Grandier glanced toward the rear end of the car. He couldn't tell if shots had pierced the tank, or if it had been damaged when he hit the wall, but it was plainly leaking now. The fumes were all around him. It would only take one spark, and—

He didn't see the bullet, but it seemed that way, a kind of freeze-frame, with the flash off to his left somewhere, a whoosh of sound behind him, then the flames were everywhere. He had to move before the fuel tank blew, but moving was a mortal danger, too, with the fire making him an easy target for his enemies.

No choice.

The sergeant came out firing, trying to count his shots, but it was hopeless. With six or seven guns against him, firing all at once, how could he count the times he pulled the trigger? A wall of heat was behind him, forcing him to hurry, running with his shoulders hunched like an old man, but he couldn't escape the bullets swarming all around him like mosquitoes.

One ripped through his shoulder, staggered him, and Grandier lurched like a drunkard, fighting for his balance, when another clipped his leg. He went down on one knee, still firing, and he barely heard the gas tank when it blew. The flames enveloped him, caught in his clothes and hair, the sudden white-hot pain investing him with strength to rise and walk.

How many bullets were left?

He didn't know or care. He couldn't see, heard nothing but the rush of hungry flames, smelled nothing but the reek of roasting meat.

A moment later, when the bullet drilled his forehead, darkness was a sweet relief.

13

Tom Carlisle took another "break" at shortly after midnight, to touch base with Jean Grandier. It was a long shot, granted, that the officer would still be working, but he thought it would be better, checking out the office first, before he started calling Grandier at home. It was a quirky kind of protocol for working cops, the recognition that his contact had a private life that wouldn't be disturbed, unless, of course, it was absolutely necessary.

It still felt strange to Carlisle, operating with a foot in each world, so to speak. On one hand, he was still an agent of the DEA, still sworn to uphold all the rules and regulations normally associated with a federal law enforcement job. But on the other hand, he had become a rogue somewhere along the way, and he was killing people in the absence of sufficient legal evidence to warrant their arrest, assuming they were even in his jurisdiction to begin with. Haiti was another story, and Carlisle didn't even want to think about it now...except that he was in the middle of it, and he had no choice.

He tapped out Grandier's number on his mobile telephone and waited for an answer. Someone picked up on the fourth ring, answering in French, and Carlisle took a shot at a Jamaican accent when he asked for Sergeant Grandier.

"Um, I'm afraid he's not available just now."

"Has he gone home?"

"Who's this calling, please?"

"A friend. I be visiting this weekend, and he's tellin' me to call him when I be there."

"I'm afraid there's been…an accident. The sergeant has, I mean to say, he's—"

"Spit it out!"

Carlisle listened to some scuffling noises on the other end, supplanted by a new voice on the line.

"Who is this calling?" the new voice demanded.

"None of your damned business."

Tom Carlisle's hands were trembling as he switched off the mobile phone, concentrating on the narrow street. Someone had blown the sergeant's cover somehow, and had killed him just like that, without a second thought. If they were killing members of the Haitian national police, no one was safe.

He tried to shrug off the sense of guilt, but there was no escaping it. The sergeant's death was his fault, any way you sliced it. No one else had called Jean Grandier out from behind his desk and placed him in the line of fire. Whatever happened after their first meeting, even though the sergeant pitched in voluntarily, the guilt came back to Carlisle. It was worse than when his partner died, in fact, because Jean Grandier had been a bystander, well insulated from the action. It was Carlisle who had dragged him into the arena, and he knew this feeling—sadness, mixed with burning rage—would stay with him until the day he died.

Which still might be today, tomorrow at the latest, if he didn't watch his ass.

Carlisle snapped out of it and reached out for the mobile phone. He had to pass the word along ASAP, and find out how Belasko wanted to respond.

Whatever he decided, Carlisle promised to himself, there would be hell to pay.

"YOU'RE SAFE, Claude. There's no reason to be frightened any longer."

"Oh?" Claude Manigat was outraged by the fact that Devereaux would speak to him as if he were a child. "Am I the only one who watches television now? Do you possess a radio? The violence is continuing, I think. I understand that a policeman has been killed."

"And what is that to you?" the master *houngan* asked.

"I'm a target for these people," Manigat replied. "Have you forgotten that, as well?"

"My memory is excellent," Devereaux said. "You're being taken care of, I believe."

"Locked up in this apartment like a prisoner," the politician whined. "It is humiliating for a man in my position."

"Who knows where you are?" the *houngan* asked.

"No one but yourself and the men outside."

"There's no humiliation, then, except in your own mind."

"But I have duties to perform, official functions to attend."

"You're taking off tomorrow, as it is, while they repair your office, and then you have the weekend. This unpleasantness will all be done by Monday morning, I assure you."

"Monday?" Manigat imagined three more days and nights shut up in the apartment, but his mind kept coming back to the alternative. With that afternoon's events in mind, it was too easy for Manigat to picture himself on the floor of his office, with bits of his skull blown away, blood and brains staining the wall.

"How can you know it will be settled?" he asked Devereaux, some of the anger draining from his voice.

"I have my methods," Devereaux replied. "You trust me, don't you, Claude?"

The special secretary almost laughed aloud at that. It

would have never crossed his mind to trust a man like Eduard Devereaux, and yet his life was in the *houngan*'s hands.

"Of course," he said a beat too late for it to sound sincere.

"I hope so. You need your friends around you at a time like this."

"I understand."

"That's good. I'll be in touch, Claude. Try to get some sleep."

The line went dead before he had a chance to speak, and Manigat returned the telephone receiver to its cradle.

Who was Eduard Devereaux to speak to *him* that way? A thief and drug dealer, no less, but Manigat had taken money from him—lots of money—and they had been allies of a sort for several years now. Devereaux knew all his secrets, and he could make life difficult for Manigat, if he was so inclined. He could kill Manigat, if it came down to that, but the politician had no fear on that score. The *houngan* wasn't one to kill the goose who laid the golden eggs. It was a great advantage to him, owning highly placed officials in the government, and if he murdered Manigat, it meant that he would have to break in a new one, risk the rejection and potential losses if he stumbled on an honest man by accident.

The special secretary knew what he had to do. If he would save himself, he had to shed the civilized exterior that he had cultivated in his long climb from the streets to a position of authority. He had to get the killer instinct back, the anger and determination that had led him to that planter's darkened bedroom with a bolo knife when he was still a child. As he had fought to help his mother then, so he had to be prepared to fight to help himself now.

Survival of the fittest was the only rule that really counted in a world of predators and prey. If Manigat had softened over time, it was a trend he could reverse with willpower. He had learned a vital lesson from his recent brush with death. There was no "civilized" society. Men played by different rules in different situations, but the toughest of them still did anything that they could get away with, when the referees weren't looking.

Manigat had been a gentleman too long.

The gloves were coming off, before it was too late.

IT TOOK TEN MINUTES to confirm Carlisle's report and verify that Sgt. Jean Grandier, assigned to drug enforcement with the Haitian national police, had been assassinated on the street. Investigation was continuing, there were no suspects at the present time...the usual.

"I'm sorry," Bolan said, and meant it. Grim experience had taught him what the DEA man had to be feeling. Bolan didn't even want to think about the friendly ghosts who sometimes came to visit him in dreams.

"It's not your fault," Carlisle said. "This shit comes down to *me*, you know? I brought him into this. He figured he was helping out the agency, and now he's dead. My fault."

"The killer's fault," Bolan corrected him. "You didn't set him up, you didn't pull the trigger."

"Hell, no. All I did was to stick him down there at the wrong end of the firing range, and tell him he should hang around awhile, I'll be right back."

"That kind of risk comes with the job." It was the truth, of course, but Bolan knew damned well no words of his would take the hurt away.

"I want to make it right," Carlisle said. "Now, I know nothing can bring him back, but I'd feel better if we kicked somebody's ass right quick, you follow me?"

"Sounds like a plan," Bolan agreed.

"What I'd really like," the Fed went on, "is to find out who set him up. One of those crooked bastards on the force, I wouldn't be surprised."

"I don't do cops," Bolan said. It had been a private rule from the beginning of his one-man holy war, and he wasn't about to change it as an antidote for someone else's grief.

"That's cool," Carlisle replied. "If I get a name and face, the bastard's history, know what I'm sayin'?"

"I'd be very much surprised to learn the triggers didn't work for Eduard Devereaux," Bolan said.

"And I want them, too. Damned right." Tom Carlisle's face was etched into a stolid mask.

"I'll see what I can do," the Executioner replied.

"It makes you think," Carlisle said. "I mean, what have I been doing all this time? I lock guys up for dealing shit, and then some mouthpiece cuts a deal to get them off, time served, a fine, whatever. You talk about the war on drugs. Congress stiffens penalties and cuts our funding in the same damned bill. They pass a law, three strikes and out, some judge in California says he won't enforce the law no matter what, because it isn't fair to criminals. Give me a break. You got the right idea, man. I'm just sorry that it took me so damned long to smell the coffee."

Bolan recognized the symptoms of frustration, disillusionment and anger, but his schedule didn't give him any time for coddling the man. Carlisle could feel sorry for the world—or for himself— when they were done in Port-au-Prince.

"You want another crack at Devereaux," he said, "we've still got work to do."

"Say when. I'm there."

"I'm thinking we should turn the heat up," Bolan said, "make Devereaux decide if he'll stay put or run for cover. While we're at it, we could pay another visit to his friend from the interior department."

"Now you're talking. I've never been that fond of politicians, if you want to know the truth."

"We'll have to find him first."

"There may be someone I can ask," the Fed replied.

"At DEA?"

Carlisle was nodding as he spoke. "I figure they might try to reel me in, but what the hell. I got no future with the agency, regardless, after this."

"Don't be so sure. There's still no reason for them to connect you with what's happened here."

"They aren't *that* stupid," Carlisle said. "Well, some of them, at least."

"You might not want to burn those bridges," Bolan suggested.

"It's hard to see much choice after the past two days."

"It doesn't have to be a life-style," Bolan said. "Think twice about that, while you're at it."

"I've been thinking," Carlisle said. "I just don't know."

"That could be a decision in itself."

"I need to make that call." The DEA agent reached for his mobile telephone.

The Executioner said nothing while the man tapped out a number and waited, started to speak in a low-pitched voice. There was no point in eavesdropping. Whatever information Carlisle gleaned from his connection he would pass along, and they could act on it together—or the Fed could always try one on his own.

Whatever, Bolan thought, the war was heating up in Port-au-Prince, and it was time to pull out all the stops. The master *houngan* and his upper-crust associates were swiftly running out of time.

As for the dark gods who protected them, well, Bolan was about to find out how they fared in open combat, when their powers were arrayed against cold steel and cleansing fire.

DAMBALLAH SEEMED to have no answers for him at the moment, forcing Eduard Devereaux to plan his own defenses from the grass roots upward. It wasn't a problem—he had always been a fighter, deadly in the clinches—but he would have felt more comfortable, admittedly, with the *loas* arrayed behind him when he met his enemy.

No matter.

Part of faith was knowing when the gods desired for you to help·yourself. If this was such a time, he could not fail. It was important that he have faith in himself, as well. Initial setbacks didn't mean that he had to lose the war, by any means. He still had hope, still had his guns and soldiers—most of them—and friends in lofty places. There were many in the Haitian government who knew that Devereaux could take them with him if he fell, and it was in their own best interest to assist him now.

He had a promise of cooperation from Paul Thibideux, to start with, and it wasn't the lieutenant's fault that Devereaux's assault team had killed Grandier before they had a chance to question him. The leader of the team had already been punished for that failure, his successor understanding that no more fiascoes would be tolerated. Fear could be instructive when selectively applied, and Eduard Devereaux never let subordinates grow overconfident when they were failing on the job.

One picture could be worth a thousand words, and so, one death could motivate a thousand men.

He still had no clear-cut idea whom he was looking for, no ID on the enemy who had been dogging him since early afternoon. The master *houngan* had competitors, of course—he didn't own the Haitian drug trade, though he had corralled the lion's share, of late—but none of those who still survived had the ambition or the nerve to risk a shooting war, much less a confrontation with his voodoo powers, on the scale that he had lately witnessed.

No, it had to be someone else, a stranger from the outside world.

That made him think about Philippe Bouchet again, and wonder if Bouchet's demise in the United States could be related to the present storm in Haiti. It defied coincidence to think that two such outbreaks, unrelated, could occur within as many days, but the idea of a connection still brought Devereaux no closer to his enemies.

He needed faces, names, perhaps a government affiliation that would tell him where to look and how he should respond.

No, scratch that. There could be no doubt upon the latter score. Once he had found the men responsible for his embarrassment, they would be killed. If he could capture them alive, so much the better; he would first question them, find out who they were working for, before he sent their worthless souls to feed Damballah. Otherwise, if he was forced to kill them on the street, like rabid dogs, he would be satisfied.

But it would leave loose ends and potential danger in the future if he didn't trace the madness to its source. If he possessed the proper information, Devereaux could take steps to eliminate the threat, no matter where he had to go or what he had to do. If it required a trip to Washington, some special demonstration of his powers to the American unbelievers who would try to put him out of business, that was fine. The master *houngan* honestly believed there were no limits to his power in the earthly realm, as long as he was favored by Damballah.

But Damballah, not unlike the weaker Christian god, still favored those who helped themselves.

All right, then, Devereaux decided, he *would* help himself. The first thing he would do toward that end was put some space between himself and his elusive enemies. He could direct the business just as well from his retreat, near Jacmel, as he could from downtown Port-au-Prince. His men knew what to do, and they would follow orders whether he was breathing down their necks or issuing instructions from a distance. Anyone who failed him knew the penalty, and wouldn't be inclined to sacrifice himself.

He thought of taking Manigat along, but instantly dismissed the notion. The politician was a pathetic whiner, self-absorbed and almost childlike in his need for constant reassurance. Devereaux had more-important problems on his hands and didn't have the time to baby a man who was supposed to be among the highest-ranking ministers of state.

Problems like living through another night, preserving all that he had worked for in the past three decades, shoring up his reputation in the face of damage he had suffered recently. If the attacks kept up, and he didn't respond effectively, there would be those among his weaker competition who would begin to think that they could challenge him, insult him with impunity. That would be bad for business, bad for all concerned.

Before he let that happen, Devereaux would see the streets of Port-au-Prince run red with blood.

But first, he would pull back, regroup and see what he could gain by looking at his problem from a distance. It would do him good, might even save his life.

And when the smoke cleared, he would be in charge, like always. He was still the master *houngan;* there was no one fit to challenge him in Haiti, no one in the world.

Damballah would provide him with the strength he needed to prevail and crush his enemies, no matter who they were or where they came from.

It was destiny.

And who was he to argue with the gods?

14

It was a replay of New Orleans: Carlisle needed information, and he had no time to waste. There were at least three angles of attack, but two of them—the DEA and Haitian national police—were closed to him by circumstances he couldn't control. His one and only contact on the local force was dead, and any contact with his own team, at the moment, would result in questions Carlisle couldn't answer, orders he couldn't obey.

Which left Plan C.

They knew Claude Manigat was part of Eduard Devereaux's machine. It was possible, then, that Devereaux would have at least some passing interest in the politician's safety, perhaps providing watchdogs or a place to hide. In any case, it stood to reason that the master *houngan*—and at least some of his men—would know where Manigat was hiding out, and that was Carlisle's goal: to track down the special secretary and scratch him off the list of Haitian power brokers, permanently.

Where it got a little tricky, though, was where to start asking questions. Some flunky shooter off the street might talk, all right—hell, he might even make things up, to spare himself some pain—but it would all be useless information. Devereaux wouldn't trust any of his low-ranked soldiers with the kind of information that could doom a major ally. On the other hand, a snatch on one of Devereaux's top guns wouldn't be feasible for Carlisle if he was acting on his own. He had prepared himself, mentally, for the prospect of death in this cause, but that didn't mean he was anxious to flush his life down the toilet with nothing to show for it.

His final choice, selected from the files Jean Grandier had passed along before he died, was one Richard Langois. If Eduard Devereaux had ranked his men with military titles, Langois would have been a master sergeant, more or less, in charge of some logistics, handling certain troops, conveying orders from the brass down to the grunts. More to the point, he was the *houngan*'s chief coordinator of security, and hence a likely prospect to be in the know if Devereaux had people guarding Manigat.

The snatch was complicated by conditions in the city, after all the shooting in the past twelve hours. Langois wasn't at home, so Carlisle tried the dance club he frequented, and came up empty once again. That left only two possibilities that Carlisle was aware of from the files, and he wasn't prepared to tackle Devereaux's headquarters on his own.

He tried the girlfriend's house instead.

You had to give Jean Grandier due credit for attention to detail. He had the woman's name and address, photographs, the days and hours when Langois—a single man who took his business seriously—would most likely seek diversion of the female kind. This night wasn't a regular appointment, granted, but Carlisle would have bet his pension that the long day's stress would need an outlet, either on the firing line or in the bedroom. And since Langois had no human targets readily available, well, it was worth a shot at least.

He found the neighborhood, parked close enough to the apartment that he wouldn't have to wander aimlessly through darkened streets to find his man. His Browning autoloader had a sound suppressor attached, with a custom-tailored shoulder rig designed to carry extra weight and let him draw at something close to normal speed. His other weapon was a blackjack, braided leather over spring steel and a knob of lead that could subdue or kill, depending on the user's upper-body strength and personal enthusiasm for his work.

There was no doorman in the lobby of the small apartment building, no visible security devices. In a neighborhood like this, you got a basic, no-frills layout for your money, nothing that would make Richard Langois stand out as Daddy Warbucks, but his monthly income still outstripped the yearly take for sixty-five percent of Haiti's population.

Carlisle used the elevator, conscious of the fact that time was slipping through his fingers, driven by a sense that even seconds counted now. On the third floor, he had the dingy hallway to himself, checked numbers on the doors to left and right and made his way down to apartment 306. The sound of reggae music emanated from behind the door and covered any voices from within.

Carlisle ran through his options, finally deciding that it wouldn't do for him to kick the door in and thereby possibly attract hostile neighbors when he needed time alone with Langois. If there was shooting, the sound suppressor would cover his end of the action, but he didn't want to waste rounds on the lock, thus giving Langois time to run and his girlfriend time to scream.

The picks were easy, though it got on Carlisle's nerves, this working in a public hallway, when a neighbor could have wandered past at any time. The reggae music covered any fumbling noise he might have made, and he was finally rewarded by the soft click of the tumblers falling into place. He pocketed the lock picks, drew his gun and let himself inside.

The music came from a stereo that would have been a fifty-dollar bargain at a swap meet in the States. Its audience had vacated the smallish living room, but Carlisle heard them panting in the bedroom, on his left. He moved in that direction, eased across the threshold, feeling for the light switch with his left hand, holding steady on the Browning with his right.

The woman was on top and doing fine, from Carlisle's point of view. She lost her rhythm when the lights came on, uncoupled from the stout man lying on his back beneath her, swiveling to face the door. Instead of screaming when she saw the gun in Carlisle's hand, the woman hissed and launched herself at the intruder, fingers hooked like talons. Carlisle's left fist met her with a rising uppercut and pitched her backward, sprawling across her playmate's legs.

Langois was fumbling for a weapon in the top drawer of the nightstand, but he never made it. Carlisle crossed the room in three quick strides and gave the drawer a solid kick that slammed it on the gunman's fingers. Langois gave a high-pitched yelp and fell back on the bed, holding his wounded hand against his chest.

"I'm hoping you speak English, brother," Carlisle said.

"I do," the Haitian replied in a quavery voice.

"Good, because we need to have a little talk."

THE DEVEREAUX ESTATE was one mile north of Port-au-Prince, just far enough outside the city to maintain a rural ambience, distinct and separate from the teeming capital. It was the kind of place "new" money often built in an attempt to mask ill-gotten gains with mock respectability. It might not be precisely true, as someone said, that all great fortunes had their roots in crime, but wholesale violation of the law had certainly become a ticket out of poverty for hundreds, maybe thousands, of disgruntled Third World people. With a little nerve, some raw intelligence and total disregard for human life, a man could claw his way out of the slums and build a palace for himself with blood money as a memorial to his achievement.

Bolan scaled the wall at the rear of Devereaux's property, tossing an army-surplus blanket across the shards of broken glass embedded in concrete along the top edge of the wall, and dropped into a crouch on manicured grass. The place was dark and quiet, just a few lights showing from the house, and while the hour could account for that, it had a different feel to Bolan.

Vacancy. Nobody home.

That wasn't absolutely accurate. He had been all of ninety seconds on the ground before he spied a sentry making the rounds. The guy was carrying an AK-47, but the way he wore it, slung across one shoulder with the muzzle pointed at the ground, he seemed to think of it as excess baggage.

Fine.

If there was one guard on the property, there should be more, which meant the careless sentry was expendable.

His target made it easy, stopping by a square-cut hedge to relieve himself. The Executioner came up behind him, looped an arm around the sentry's neck and gave a twist that crushed his larynx, separating vertebrae before the gunman had a notion as to what was happening.

He tucked the body out of sight behind the hedge, taking the Kalashnikov along as backup just in case his estimate of guards on tap fell on the low side of reality. No one stepped out to challenge him as he approached the house, and Bolan made a hasty circuit of the mansion, peering in through ground-floor windows where the draperies were open, quickly verifying his impression that the master *houngan* wasn't home.

The second guard was sitting in a lawn chair on the porch. It occurred to Bolan that the shooters might have been forbidden access to the house, or maybe they had orders to remain outside and on alert while it was dark, catch up on sack time in the daylight, when there would be less risk of attack. Whatever, Bolan knew this man, with the riot shotgun lying on the porch beside his chair, might be his last chance to find out where Eduard Devereaux had gone.

He took no chances, climbing silently across the railing of the porch, approaching from his target's blind side. In a moment, he was close enough to stand with one foot on the shotgun, while the muzzle of his liberated AK-47 pressed against the gunman's neck.

"Relax," he said. "Do you speak English?"

"*Oui,*" the lookout answered, then reckoned he should prove it. "Yes, I do."

"Good deal. I have one question for you. You can live or die, your choice."

"What is the question?"

"Where's your boss?"

The sentry thought about it, looking for a way to save himself without incurring even greater danger somewhere down the line. At last, he said, "You must not tell him where you got the information."

"He won't hear from me."

The young man hesitated for another ten or fifteen seconds, then he said, "Jacmel. You know it?"

"On the coast," Bolan said. "South."

"There is a house outside the city, on the coastal highway. West of Jacmel, in the hills."

"How far?"

"From here?"

"From Jacmel," Bolan said.

"Perhaps two miles. No more than three."

"When did he leave?"

"Two hours, maybe less."

"Okay, that's it."

He stepped back, freeing up the shotgun, walking backward toward the point where he had crawled across the railing. At the final moment, Bolan turned his back, ears perked to catch the scuffling sound that was inevitable.

There was no way the young man could let him walk,

unless the sentry planned to spend his life in hiding, waiting for one of the master *houngan*'s men to tap him on the shoulder.

Bolan let him reach the shotgun and lift it, before he turned and stroked the AK-47's trigger. Half a dozen rounds ripped through his target's chest and stomach, punched him backwards, flattening the lawn chair as he fell.

All done.

The Executioner stood waiting for a moment, just in case he was mistaken and they had some backup dozing in the house, but no one came in answer to the sound of gunfire. He retraced his steps across the darkened grounds and dropped the rifle at the point where he had scaled the wall. An easy up-and-over, with a hundred yards of open ground ahead, before he reached his waiting car.

It gave him time to think about the long drive south, to Jacmel. It could easily turn out to be another trap, like Bouchet's island off the Mississippi coast, but Bolan couldn't let his adversary slip away so easily.

If Devereaux was leading him, the Executioner would let himself be led.

It was the only game in town, and he had come to play.

THE HOUSE outside Jacmel was more modest than his home near Port-au-Prince, but Eduard Devereaux enjoyed it all the same. A two-room bungalow would have been more luxurious than any home he was familiar with while growing up, and this one was considerably larger, with its sauna, five bedrooms and the basement that he had converted into a ritual chamber to practice his art. The house stood on a twenty-acre plot, with trees surrounding it on three sides—north, east, west—and the Caribbean due south, a panoramic view that was among the most spectacular of any on the island.

Devereaux enjoyed the time he spent here by himself, a few days now and then, when he could tear himself away from business for a while. It did him good, restored his energy, reminding him that life wasn't composed entirely of the city lights and grubbing after dollars in the drug trade. He wasn't ashamed of how he earned his living, or the way in which he served Damballah, but it grated on his nerves sometimes, the constant planning for security against potential enemies, the conversations with accountants, rubbing shoulders with the human scum who gravitated toward the world of politics.

The present crisis was unusual, but it wasn't the first time Eduard Devereaux had wound up fighting for his life. So far, he had prevailed in those encounters, and he had no reason to believe that he would lose this time. His unnamed enemies were more determined than the usual, but they were only human, after all. They would have weaknesses he could exploit. Damballah would assist him, if he asked the proper questions, showed the proper degree of humility in his approach to the Great Serpent. No man could defeat Damballah or his servants if the Serpent joined in opposition to their plans.

The master *houngan* knew that he wasn't invincible, but he had powers other men didn't possess. With the assistance of Damballah, he was more than equal to the latest challenge of his enemies. And he hadn't been running when he turned his back on Port-au-Prince. Instead, he was retreating to a more strategic vantage point, where he could work his magic, lay his snares and wait for those who hunted him.

If they pursued him to Jacmel, they would be coming to their deaths. Damballah had already promised him. The Serpent didn't lie.

It would be interesting to meet the men who wished him dead and crush them underneath his feet like crawling insects. A refreshing change from the embarrassment he had experienced of late, in the United States and Port-au-Prince.

Lieutenant Thibideux was driving down from Port-au-

Prince within the hour to coordinate defensive preparations at the Jacmel hardsite. He couldn't supply police for Devereaux's protection, but he was an old hand at detecting weakness in the kind of layout that the *houngan* was preparing for his enemies. It would be good for Thibideux to get out of the city for a while and earn his money in the field, instead of simply sitting at a desk and making phone calls all day long.

Together, they would beat these strangers who had dared to challenge Eduard Devereaux. With some assistance from Damballah, they would grind the upstarts into dust and scatter them at sea.

RICHARD LANGOIS HAD spilled his guts, believing it would save him. He was wrong, of course—Carlisle couldn't afford to leave the man alive to warn their target, once he had disgraced himself by telling tales. A warning call to Manigat would be the least of it; Langois could easily have rallied troops to help defend the special secretary, maybe spoiling everything.

"I had to dust him," Carlisle stated, with no emotion showing on his face or in his voice. "The woman cut out."

"It happens," Bolan said.

They sat a half block from Manigat's apartment, on the far side of the street, having surveyed the target with a drive-by moments earlier. The guards were right where Langois had predicted they would be, both sitting in the car, across from the apartment building that had no entrance from the rear.

"Be ready when I take them," Bolan said. "We need to wrap this up and hit the road."

"I'll take them," Carlisle said, correcting him. "You're better on the point, in case the guy was leading me on, and they've got someone else on the inside."

Bolan considered it and nodded. Carlisle had his reasons,

and the motivation made no difference to Bolan if the job got done.

"Okay," he agreed, and stepped out of the car, Carlisle unloading on the driver's side. He crossed the street, while the DEA agent moved along the sidewalk, northbound, coming up behind the compact with the gunners in it, walking with the silenced Browning in his hand, pressed flat against his thigh. Bolan didn't keep pace with Carlisle, but let him pull out in front. It was important that the guards be taken down before he reached the small apartment building, so they were not alerted by a stranger idling on the stoop.

He watched and waited, saw Carlisle come up behind the car and stop, his pistol rising, orange flame darting from the muzzle as the Browning whispered death from six or seven feet away. There was no answer from the vehicle, his targets slumping forward, dead before they were aware of danger closing on their blind side.

Quick and clean.

He started walking faster, stepped into the lobby just as Carlisle crossed the street to join him. There were no pedestrians about to see them and go running off to call police. Claude Manigat was three floors up, presumably alone, and clueless to the proximity of Death.

They climbed the stairs together, side by side, paced off the hallway to the special secretary's door. The place was silent at that hour of the night, no babies crying, nothing in the way of sounds from radio or television. Bolan guessed their target would be sleeping, but he had to keep in mind the fact that Manigat could just as easily be sitting up, prepared to fight, not trusting those downstairs who had already let him down.

"On me," Bolan said.

"Right."

He kicked the door in, followed in a rush, with Carlisle close behind him. There was no one in the living room or tiny kitchen. Double-timing down a short hall, past the dark and silent bathroom, Bolan saw two other doors, one straight ahead, the other on his right. He pointed toward the right-hand door and kept on going, slamming through the farther one, momentum taking him across the threshold while Carlisle checked the other sleeping room.

A lamp was coming on as Bolan cleared the doorway, Manigat lurching up in bed and groping for a pistol on the nightstand. He was speaking rapid-fire, excited French, and while it meant nothing to Bolan, there was no mistaking his intent. The special secretary had his weapon now, and he was turning toward the doorway, thumbing back the hammer, trying desperately to aim.

The Glock jumped twice in Bolan's fist, a pair of bullets homing on the special secretary's chest. They slammed him back against the headboard of his bed, the shiny autoloader tumbling from his fingers as his eyes rolled backward in his head and he went limp.

And it was over, just like that.

"In here," Bolan said, hearing Carlisle approach as soon as he had checked out the empty second bedroom. They spent a moment staring at the dead man, watching blood soak through the satin sheets he had to have purchased to impress a woman, once upon a time.

So much for romance, and a promising political career. Claude Manigat had bet his life on worthless friends, and he had paid the tab in blood.

"Looks like we're finished here," Carlisle said.

"Looks like."

"Okay. I'll drive."

The trip to Jacmel had been Eduard Devereaux's idea, and while Paul Thibideux resented the summons that drew him away from his office in Port-au-Prince, there had been no way to turn him down. He still depended on the *houngan* for sixty percent of his income, all tax free, and there was more to be afraid of than a simple drop in revenue if he defied a man possessed of Devereaux's powers.

So he had come running, albeit out of uniform, to check on the security arrangements at the Jacmel house. Thibideux recognized his appearance as a sign of obedience more than anything else. Devereaux had professional killers and security technicians on his payroll; he didn't require a member of the Haitian national police to walk around the grounds and double-check his gun emplacements, as if Thibideux were grading the performance of a class in boot camp. It was ego, the *houngan* flexing his muscles for personal amusement and the edification of his troops, showing all concerned that he was still in charge, still pulling strings.

Thibideux had learned to live with the embarrassment, thinking first of his Bahamian bank account when he felt the anger heating up his face, provoking him to make some rash remark. He imagined himself with a new identity, relaxing on a shady veranda in some other country, far beyond the *houngan*'s reach.

Or maybe, not so far.

The way things had been going, up to now, there was at

least an outside chance that Devereaux wouldn't survive
the present crisis. It was hard to grasp, at one level, but
Devereaux's powers had done little for him in the contest
with his enemies. It almost seemed as if Damballah had
deserted him to meet his fate alone. Could that be possible?
And if it was, what would it mean to men like Thibideux,
who had been ruled by dictates from the master *houngan*
for so long?

The lieutenant wasn't concerned about the prospect of
finding himself another patron in the underworld. There had
always been crime in Haiti, and criminals with money had
always paid off the police. There was no reason to expect
that that would change, and while the honored tradition
continued, Thibideux would be standing by to claim his
share of the booty.

The trick, if Devereaux went down, would be for Thibideux to avoid getting caught in the whirlpool effect,
sucked down to his doom with the rest. Granted, his tour
of the Jacmel estate wasn't the best way to put distance
between himself and Devereaux, but he still had to go
through the motions, preserve the facade of loyalty, in case
Devereaux managed to pull it out at the last moment, save
himself and come back strong.

Stranger things had happened in Haiti, with or without
the interference of the gods.

The main thing now was to inform Devereaux of his
conclusions, rubber-stamp the preparations now in place
around the house and grounds, then drive straight back to
Port-au-Prince before—

His train of thought was interrupted by a single shot,
almost immediately followed by a burst of automatic-
weapons fire. Thibideux cursed Devereaux's men, damned
fools jumping at shadows...and then he felt a chill race
down his spine.

Suppose the enemy had followed Devereaux from Port-
au-Prince, tracked him down and organized a fresh assault?

In that case, there would be no time to waste. Thibideux had to find out what was happening and get himself away from there before police arrived. There would be no good explanation for his presence at the house, no way to shield himself, if he was swept up in a dragnet.

Or if he was killed.

The prospect chilled him, and he started running toward the house with no thought for decorum, long strides eating up the lawn. He had to see Devereaux, then get out of there without delay.

He only hoped that it wasn't too late.

A DRIVE-BY HAD SHOWN Bolan all that he could see of his intended target without going in on foot. There was a wall around the grounds, with sentries on the wrought-iron gate in front, lights showing from the house beyond a screen of trees. The DEA had aerial-surveillance photographs, for all the good it did them in a foreign country, and Carlisle had sketched the layout from memory, creating a fairly detailed battle map.

Two men couldn't surround an enemy, unless the two of them had access to advanced technology that wasn't presently available to Bolan and his ally from the DEA. In the absence of space-age hardware, they would have to make do with old-fashioned guts and determination, shaving the odds by any means at their disposal, concentrating on the central figure of the drug cartel and dealing with his soldiers as they came.

They found a place to leave the car a half mile past the walled estate, concealed within a copse of trees set well back from the coastal highway. Working swiftly, they changed into camouflage fatigues and armed themselves, each with a folding stock Kalashnikov, spare magazines, grenades and the side arms they had carried since arriving on the island. In addition to his other hardware, Bolan had a satchel filled with plastique charges, and a pouch of timers on his belt. Carlisle waited while he dabbed his face and hands with war paint to eliminate the glare from any errant moonbeams.

Ready.

Hiking back, Bolan left his comrade on the west side of the property and kept on going, following the wall until he reached the eastern side, directly opposite. The wall had coils of razor wire on top, and Bolan used the blanket trick again, felt sharp steel poking at him through the layers of wool as he went up and over, dropping safely on the other side.

The trees helped cover his approach, but there were also men among them, hunting singly and in pairs, prepared to deal with any prowlers they discovered on the grounds. The first one Bolan met was on his own, a twenty-something gunner with an M-1 carbine in his hands. It didn't help him when a strong hand sealed his lips and twisted, sending white-hot spikes of agony into his brain before a knife blade followed, plunged in to the hilt and instantly withdrew.

The man went limp in Bolan's arms, deadweight. It took a moment to conceal his body in among the nearby ferns, but thirty seconds saw him back on course and heading for the house. He met another lookout ninety seconds later, coming through the trees and concentrating on the ground in front of him, as if afraid that he might fall. While he was concentrating on his feet, the barrel of an AK-47 slammed into his face and pitched him over backward, grunting like a stunned pig as he fell.

The killing blow was simple, with a sharp jab to the larynx as his target lay there, thrashing on the grass. Death was instantaneous and silent, choking off the gunner's voice and breath at once, while Bolan jerked the shotgun from his spastic hands and held it out of reach.

Another body went into the undergrowth, and Bolan started picking up his pace to compensate for the brief interruptions. Carlisle should be well inside the grounds by now, and safe—the lack of gunfire so far told him that much—and they were supposed to reach the house together, more or less. Precision was a goal that every soldier strove for, and that few achieved in combat situations, but the timing grew increasingly critical as hostile odds increased. If he was late, and Carlisle had to go in on his own...

The sentry loomed in front of Bolan, interrupting conscious thought. Instinct took over, the Executioner slashing with a boot in the direction of his adversary's groin, the AK-47 swinging toward a startled face. The skinny gunman staggered, jets of blood exploding from his broken nose, but he was tougher than he looked. He didn't fall at once, but rather tried to raise the submachine gun he was carrying in an attempt to save himself.

Too late.

A second kick disarmed him, and it made no difference when the Haitian threw up an arm to protect his wounded face. The solar plexus made an equally inviting target, and Bolan jabbed with the muzzle of his weapon, ready when the gunman doubled over, stepping back to kick him squarely in the face, as if his head had been a soccer ball. There was an outside chance his vertebrae were still intact, and Bolan was prepared to finish it, already moving forward in a crouch, when sudden movement at the corner of his left eye made him spin in that direction to confront another sentry well beyond his reach.

The frightened-looking gunner fired a pistol shot, hands jerking so the shot went high and wide. There was no point in rushing him, no time to do it right, and Bolan answered with a 3-round burst that slammed him over backward, dead before his shoulders hit the lawn.

And there went any hope of sneaking up on Eduard Devereaux.

Thinking briefly of Tom Carlisle, hoping he was safe,

the Executioner allowed himself one bitter curse and started sprinting toward the house.

THE SHOOTING STARTLED Eduard Devereaux. He was expecting it, but that was at some abstract level, where he imagined that his enemies would walk into the trap like cattle moving through a slaughterhouse, perhaps with warning from his guards on the perimeter to let him watch and savor their annihilation. When the first shots sounded, coming out of nowhere in the darkness, it occurred to him that some fool might have fired on Thibideux, but then he realized the very notion was preposterous. His enemies had found him, sooner than the *houngan* had anticipated, and they meant to see him dead.

Others, with the same idea, had tried before, and he was still alive.

He stepped outside and saw Paul Thibideux approaching, coming toward the house at a dead run. Whatever pride was left to the lieutenant, it didn't prevent him running for his life, as if the very hounds of hell were snapping at his heels.

The pistol tucked inside Devereaux's belt, concealed by his stylish sport coat, added reassuring weight, as if to ground him where he stood. The *houngan* felt like drawing it to frighten Thibideux, but what would be the point? The officer was running scared already. He disgusted Devereaux, and there could be no benefit in keeping him around. He would be worthless in a fight, and killing him would only add another chore for the disposal crew, when they were finished mopping up the *houngan*'s enemies.

"Eduard! I can't stay here." Thibideux was panting as he reached the house. He broke stride and staggered to a jerky halt.

"Of course not," Devereaux replied. "By all means, go."

His swift agreement plainly startled Thibideux. The of-

ficer stood frowning at him for a moment, waiting for the
other shoe to drop, the punch line to be played at his ex-
pense, before he said, "You don't want me to stay?"

"Does 'go' mean 'stay'?"

"No, but—"

"You're wasting time, Paul. I, for one, cannot afford it."

Devereaux stepped past him, smiling at the officer's be-
wilderment. The moment swiftly passed, and Devereaux
put the lieutenant out of mind, as he began to concentrate
on the defensive measures he had to take. His men were
all in place supposedly, and he had called upon Damballah
for the strength they would require to see them through
what he assumed would be a brisk and bloody fight. As for
himself, he didn't plan to run and hide from those who
sought to kill him, not when he could see to the defenses
on his own and supervise the victory.

Be careful. His voice, speaking to him from the back of
his mind. He didn't need to hear it, knowing as he did the
risks involved, but it was good to know that portion of his
brain was functioning. He was not frightened yet, although
perhaps he should have been. Three dozen gunmen to protect him, plus the powers he had cultivated in his years of
studying the Art—how could he fail?

There was an echo of a gunshot in among the trees, but
Devereaux believed the shots had emanated from the east
side of the property, in the direction of Jacmel. Sound carried in the darkness, but he didn't think his nearest neighbors—close to half a mile away, at that—would waste time
calling the police. Perhaps if shooting went on long
enough...

Another reason to conclude the business with dispatch
and get the bodies cleared away. There would be time
enough to gloat about his victory when he had dealt with
all the details, wiped out every trace of opposition to his
status as the leading *houngan* and drug runner on the island.
Besides his life and property, he had a reputation to protect,

and this particular embarrassment had gone on long enough.

Too long, in fact.

Simply eliminating those who challenged him might not be good enough. The others, his potential enemies who lacked the nerve to strike so far, would need a sign to keep them in their place. Signs were a specialty of Devereaux's, and it shouldn't be difficult to think of something once the victory was his, and he had vanquished enemies with which to work. Alive or dead, it made no difference.

They would all be dead before he finished with them.

The mental picture made him smile again, as he proceeded toward the sound of gunfire, calling for his sergeant of the guard. There were last-minute preparations to be made, and he had no more time to waste.

TOM CARLISLE KNEW they had big trouble when he heard the guns go off. No matter how you sliced it, that could only be bad news. Alive or dead, Belasko had run into something unexpected, was drawing fire from someone on the home team and was firing back at them—assuming that had been his AK-47 Carlisle heard. Any chance they had of coming at the house by stealth was now blown.

It would have been a perfect time to cut and run, if he was bailing out, but Carlisle wasn't going anywhere. Whatever happened to Belasko, whether Carlisle ever saw the man alive again or not, he would continue with his mission to the bitter end.

It felt as if he had been waiting for this moment all his life.

Carlisle picked up his pace, kept moving toward the house. It struck him that Belasko's difficulty might work out to his advantage, drawing sentries from the west side of the property to find out what was cooking on the other side. He hoped so, anyway, but kept his weapon ready just in case.

When he was halfway to the house, he met a pair of gunners who were keeping to their posts despite the sounds of combat emanating from the far side of the property. It could mean they were frightened, or perhaps that they possessed a heightened sense of duty. Either way, they were a problem he would have to deal with swiftly if he meant to stay alive and do his job.

His right hand drew the Browning automatic, and he was sighting down the slide before one of the shooters saw him coming, from a range of less than thirty feet. He fired two shots and took the gawker down as if he were a rag doll, crumpling in a pile of twisted limbs and sweaty clothes, with bloodstains seeping through.

The second shooter had a 12-gauge shotgun tucked beneath his right arm, close enough that he could feel it all the time, but not the best position for a hasty draw. He fumbled with the weapon, giving Carlisle all the time he needed for a head shot, blood and brains exploding from the gunman's shattered skull.

He kept the pistol in his right hand, AK-47 in his left. If there was further silent killing to be done before he reached the house, it made no sense to holster the silenced Browning. Carlisle was thinking of his cronies in the Nashville office, wishing they could see him now, when sudden crashing in the undergrowth off to his right alerted him to danger. He swung in that direction, with the Browning braced at full arm's length, a duelling stance, and he was ready when a solitary gunman blundered into view.

The guy was either lost or running for his life, and either way, the last turn was a killer. He had time to blink at Carlisle and swing up his own Kalashnikov, then the Browning whispered twice and opened blow holes in his chest. The young man staggered, fighting to maintain his balance while the final seconds of his life ran out, and then his legs buckled, dropping him faceforward on the grass.

He still had more than half a clip in the pistol, with no

need to replace the magazine just yet. Carlisle regained his heading, picking up the pace, a quick jog through the shadows pooled among the stately trees. In California, landscaping like that would cost a fortune, and while Haitian standards scraped the bottom of the barrel when it came to calculating labor costs, the house and grounds hadn't come cheap.

The house was just ahead of him, lights shining through the trees, the sound of agitated voices telling him the troops were on alert.

He waited for a moment at the tree line. There were at least a dozen soldiers visible from where he stood, and Carlisle didn't feel like rushing them across the open lawn. If only one or two of them got lucky in the firestorm such a move would generate, it would be all she wrote for Mrs. Carlisle's little Tommy.

There had to be a better way.

He studied the detached garage, some fifty paces closer to the house and offset, to his right, so that it almost crouched against the nearby trees. If he could make it that far without being seen, he had a chance to reach the house from a new angle, let the nervous sentries mill around out front while he closed in to seek an entry from behind.

It sounded worth a try, and he was getting nowhere as it was.

He turned hard right, clutching his AK-47 tightly as he started running through the trees.

THE SOUNDS OF GUNFIRE beckoned Bolan's adversaries like a siren's song. Some of them shouted questions back and forth as they were stalking him, as if to keep him posted on their whereabouts. It was a thoughtful gesture, and he turned it to his own advantage when a group of four or five collected in the darkness somewhere to his left. The frag grenade was silent in its flight, and while he couldn't drop it in their laps with anything approaching surgical precision, he got close enough.

A clap of smoky thunder ripped the night, immediately trailed by voices wailing in the darkness, crying out in pain. He counted two survivors, wondered if the other two or three were dead or merely wounded, and dismissed the train of thought as fruitless. He wasn't required to bury every soldier on the *houngan*'s payroll, after all. One shot or one grenade could wrap up the mission, from Bolan's point of view.

But first, he had to locate Eduard Devereaux.

The house was Bolan's destination, logic telling him the *houngan* would be quartered there, perhaps attempting to conceal himself or maybe trying to escape. Carlisle had planned to take care of the cars if he had time and opportunity, but things were now happening so quickly that strategy went out the window in a rush.

Another hundred yards or so remained before he reached the house, and he would have to run a bloody gauntlet, getting there. His enemies had thrown up a defensive line of sorts, within the cultivated woods that ringed the *houngan*'s home away from home. He didn't have a fix on numbers or exact locations, but he knew the game. Manhunting in the dark had been a standard feature of his service in the military, and the Executioner had kept his hand in through the bitter contests of his private war against the savages.

If they were up for stalking, he would show them just how easily a hunter could become the prey.

He moved among them like a shadow, knife in hand, a blur of motion on the far left of the ambush line eliminating one gun from the set. His next stop was a little tricky, two men crouched together in the shadow of an ancient tree. He came up on them swiftly, silently, slugged one man with the pommel of his Ka-bar fighting knife, slashing at the other with a stroke that sent a crimson geyser spouting from beneath his chin. The first, stunned target was recovering enough to shout a warning when the blade slipped in between his ribs and twisted, sawing back and forth through veins and muscle, finally withdrawing on a scarlet tide.

He was relentless, a machine designed for killing, leaving twisted, silent bodies in his wake. None of them saw Death coming, and none got off a shot in self-defense before dying.

The next-to-last man made some noise, a dying gurgle as his throat was opened by the blade. It was enough to tip his comrade off to danger on his flank and start the gunner shooting aimlessly, no target he could fix his sights on, wasting bursts on darkness in a desperate rage to save himself.

It didn't help.

The AK-47 stuttered briefly, dead on target from a range of forty feet. It was a simple thing to aim above the shooter's muzzle-flashes, hose him down and watch his body topple in the ferns that had concealed him moments earlier.

The house was waiting—*Devereaux* was waiting—and the Executioner didn't linger on the killing ground, waiting for other adversaries to arrive. If they were hunting for him, they would have to find him on the move and take their chances, just like anybody else.

The trees were thinning out. Soon, Bolan would be stripped of cover, left to cross the final stretch of open lawn without protection. There was no point brooding over it, he realized; the risk came with the territory. If he made it, he would have a shot at Devereaux. Maybe.

Then there was Carlisle, if the sentries hadn't cornered him or gunned him down. And if they both failed, maybe somewhere down the road there would be Able Team or Phoenix Force to take the job and do it right.

The master *houngan* was as good as dead; he simply didn't know it yet. The only questions still remaining were how long he would take to die to get the message, and how many souls would he take with him when he went.

The clock was running, fast approaching sudden-death overtime. There would be no time-outs, no substitutions. Anyone who couldn't pull his weight would be cut from the team once and for all, with no recourse to any system of appeals. A few more yards, a few more minutes, and the end would be in sight.

DETACHED GARAGES always made Tom Carlisle think of luxury somehow. Size was irrelevant, per se. The very concept made a statement that the owner had enough spare land that he could easily afford to plant a second building on it, separated from his dwelling, just to house his vehicles. Where Carlisle came from, no one had garages, and the people who had cars would either park them on the street or in their yards. Outside the ghetto, where you started running into "normal" houses, they were small at first, with the garages tacked on like an afterthought, connected to the kitchen pantry by an access door that let exhaust fumes and the smell of motor oil inside the house whenever it was opened. Farther out, among the larger homes—

A bullet whispered past his ear and snapped the agent's roving mind back to reality. He hit a crouch and looked around for snipers, but he came up empty, finally accepting that the bullet had to have been a stray. Dumb luck that it had missed him, when it could as easily have struck him in the head and dropped him like a rock.

Full house, he thought as he closed in on Devereaux's detached garage and started counting cars that had been parked outside. If there were three or four cars tucked inside, and each car visible had carried four or five men to the Jacmel hardsite, it would mean that they were up against a force of close to forty guns.

He spent an extra moment checking out the garage, making sure that Devereaux didn't have any gunners hiding underneath the cars or perched up on the roof to take him by surprise. The vehicles apparently weren't an issue when it came to laying out security around the place. They were inside the wall; no one could take them out through guarded gates without approval from the boss.

No problem.

Carlisle didn't plan to take them out. He planned to blow them up.

Strategically it wouldn't count for much, but it would make one hell of a diversion when the long garage and half a dozen cars went up like giant firecrackers. If nothing else, it would distract some gunmen from the house, perhaps help clear the way for Belasko, going in. Whatever helped them pin the tag on Eduard Devereaux, they would be points ahead.

He had a couple of grenades, no real explosives like Belasko carried, but Carlisle didn't think that it would be a problem. He could open gas caps, shred his handkerchief for wicks and get the fireworks started that way. Maybe use the frag grenades for emphasis, once it got rolling, with a decent bonfire blazing in the night.

He scuttled forward in a crouch, using the nearest car for cover, screening himself from the view of any gunners on the south side of the house. The car in question was a year-old Cadillac, jet black. Carlisle was crawling toward the driver's side to ease off the gas cap, when something caught his eye about the license plate and made him do a hasty double take.

It bore the emblem of the Haitian national police.

His thoughts snapped back to Jean Grandier, the ambush that had killed him and the sense of guilt that Carlisle carried in relation to his death. He had told himself repeatedly that it hadn't been his fault, but it didn't ring true. Now, here was someone from the home team, Grandier's own department, hanging out with Devereaux...for what?

What difference did it make?

The sound of running footsteps froze him where he was, on hands and knees, until he heard them stop beside the Cadillac. There was a fumbling, jingling noise as someone dropped his keys, and Carlisle risked a glance around the fender, just in time to see a Haitian in a suit bend down to pick up his keys off the ground. The hand that reached for them was shaking, and the guy was sweating like a fat man in a sauna.

Carlisle drew the silenced Browning, had the stranger covered well before he spoke. "Don't go," he said. "This gig's just warming up."

The Haitian nearly fainted, took a jerky backward step before he saw the gun and reconsidered, freezing where he stood.

"Who are you?"

"I'm a friend of Sergeant Grandier's," Carlisle said. "Do you recognize the name?"

The guy was blinking now, so rapidly that it resembled a spasmodic facial tic. He knew the name, all right, but he wasn't about to say so.

Never mind.

"You might have heard, he had a little accident in Port-au-Prince. Somebody set him up, in fact."

"I don't know anything."

"Must make it hard to do your job, no brain and all. But, hey, no problem. I just want to give you something, from my friend."

"Your friend?"

"The sergeant, you remember?"

"Sergeant."

"There you go."

The first 9 mm round struck Carlisle's target just above the belt buckle, a crimson flower blooming on his white dress shirt. The dying man lurched backward, clutching at his gut with one hand, while the other fumbled for a weapon on his belt, but he was way too late for any kind of fast-draw action.

Carlisle let him have two more, both in the chest, and dropped the Haitian in his tracks. He waited for a rush of sweet relief that never came, a part of his mind kicking in with the snide remark that he would never know for sure who was responsible for Grandier's assassination, but ultimately it came back to Eduard Devereaux. The best thing he could do, to make things right, was to get on with business, do it right.

Tom Carlisle tucked the Browning automatic back into its shoulder rig and reached out for the gas cap of the shiny Cadillac.

THE BATTLE TIDE had shifted on him somehow, and no matter how he tried to work it out to put things right, it seemed to Eduard Devereaux that he was losing ground. His men had let him down once more, and it was possible that he would die within the next few minutes if he trusted them to cover him or help him get away.

It was humiliating, being driven out of house and home by strangers, but there was no time for anger now. Survival was his first priority. When he was safe again, there would be time enough for sorting out the problems, learning what went wrong, assigning blame and punishment. When that time came, he would be ruthless.

His first thought was to grab a driver and make a quick dash to the cars. The thought had barely taken shape when an explosion rocked the *houngan* in his tracks, immediately followed by another and another. Facing south, toward the detached garage, he saw a fireball shooting up into the sky. Some of the cars were burning, and another one exploded as he watched, streamers of burning gasoline shooting through the night like solar flares.

Too late.

His enemies were crafty—Devereaux would grant them

that. They had anticipated his move, cut him off before he could make it. There would be no escape by car, but that didn't mean he was trapped. Not yet.

"Damballah, help me!"

Devereaux's gun was in his hand before the prayer had left his lips. The Serpent would watch over him, but he couldn't expect a bolt of lightning from the heavens to destroy his enemies. Where earthly business was concerned, the gods helped out and gave advice, but they couldn't be troubled to appear in person and contend with lowly human beings.

Eduard Devereaux would have to save himself.

He turned and started back in the direction of the house.

THE HOUSEMEN WERE distracted when the cars went up like Roman candles, spreading flames to the garage, the grass and anything else that would burn within a fifty-foot radius. Bolan took advantage of the show to make his way inside the house, surprised a Haitian gunner in the dining room and left him with a fractured skull.

The action lay outside, and Devereaux's surviving men were out there in the thick of it, no doubt with orders to defend their master and his home at any cost. The ground floor was deserted, once he took care of the straggler in the dining room, and Bolan rushed upstairs to check out the bedrooms. More dead air, empty rooms that echoed with the sounds of mortal combat from outside.

He started back downstairs, disgusted that he had apparently missed Devereaux again. The man was slick, no doubt about it.

Bolan was about to exit, gamble on another look around the grounds, when the muffled sound of a voice reached his ears, some kind of chanting.

The door had stopped two inches short of closing. Maybe Devereaux was in a hurry, or perhaps he simply didn't care. Whatever, Bolan eased the door back, ready with his

AK-47, covering a flight of stairs that led down to some kind of murky basement, pale light flickering below, like candles.

Make that torches.

Bolan saw them, sticking out of sconces on the walls, when he was halfway down the stairs. Some thirty feet in front of him, a man was kneeling with his back to Bolan, moving bones and things around a low altar, chanting in a language that wasn't patois or any other dialect the Executioner had ever heard before.

He didn't stop to think who might be listening on the receiving end of all that mumbo jumbo. Bolan's fight was with a man, the man who knelt before him now, caught up in some peculiar ritual. If Eduard Devereaux was hoping he could save himself with magic, he knew nothing of his enemy.

The basement had been soundproofed, but the door was open. Bolan didn't let it stop him, since they had the big house to themselves. He brought the automatic rifle to his shoulder, aimed and fired a 3-round burst that shattered two large jars at one end of the voodoo altar. Crimson liquid splashed across the floor, and the warrior had no way of knowing whether it was blood or some facsimile. It made no difference, either way.

The *houngan* spun, then leaped to his feet. He had a shiny pistol in his right hand, pointed at the floor.

"You've come," he said.

"I hope I didn't keep you waiting."

"Not at all. I have been looking forward to it."

"We aim to please," Bolan said.

"May I ask who you are?"

"What difference does it make?" the Executioner replied.

"None, really. I just wondered if you were employed by one of my competitors. Perhaps—"

"No deals," Bolan interrupted him. "It's not a takeover."

"But then—"

"Your tab's due," Bolan said. "I'm just here to collect."

"Do you believe in magic?"

"I do," Bolan replied. "Children have magic. Every human life has magic in it, until a thing like you steps in and poisons it."

"A matter of perspective," Eduard Devereaux replied. "If you'll allow me to explain."

"Not this time," Bolan said. "Clock's running, and I didn't come to chat."

"Of course. In that case—"

Bringing up the shiny pistol, Devereaux squeezed off his first round prematurely, and the bullet ricocheted off concrete, drilled the wall somewhere in back of Bolan. The AK hammered for three seconds, bullets ripping through the master *houngan*'s chest and stomach, pitching him backward. The altar clipped him behind his knees, and Devereaux went down, the handgun spinning from his fingers, off across the basement floor.

The Haitian's lips were moving, maybe praying to his snake god, but no sound was coming out. Bolan left him to it, planting two fat plastic charges in the basement, fixing them strategically and setting their timers for a short countdown.

Upstairs, he left another charge beside the front door, pressed against the jamb, with forty seconds on the clock. From there, he made his way outside and put the house behind him, jogging toward the tree line. By the time he palmed the compact walkie-talkie, he was conscious of the fact that there was no more firing on the grounds. An eerie stillness had descended on the killing field.

"We're done here," Bolan told Carlisle, "and the house is going in approximately half a minute. Are you clear?"

"As can be," Carlisle said. "Fact is, I've plumb run out of playmates."

"So I'll meet you at the gate."

"I'm on my way."

Bolan paused beside the driveway, glanced back toward the house and waited for another moment. Any second now...

The blast lit up the grounds like the sunrise, followed by another and another, until the midnight sky was bright with cleansing fire.

"So burn," he said, and turned back toward the distant gates.

EPILOGUE

"They didn't give you any static, then?"

"Not yet. So far, so good."

Tom Carlisle wasn't smiling as he spoke, although he seemed relaxed. The coffee shop was crowded, as they had expected it to be at rush hour in Miami International's main concourse, but the man from DEA still had another forty minutes left before the boarding call for his connecting flight.

"If you wind up taking too much heat," Bolan said, "I know someone you can call."

"I'll be all right. They mostly think I've been off somewhere, grieving for my partner, maybe getting drunk or getting laid."

"So, what about Bouchet?" Bolan asked.

"That's no problem. They'll believe that he and Doobie Arnold took each other out. Shit happens in the trade, you know?"

"It works for me."

"What about yourself?" Carlisle asked. "Do you get some time off now, or what?"

"We'll see."

He was already thinking of New Orleans, stopping by to visit Marianne Lacroix to see how she was holding up after her ordeal, but he wondered if it was a good idea. He had been favored with a standing invitation, just in case he got the chance, but part of Bolan's mind was telling him that he had spent enough time in her life already—nearly ended it, in fact, by dragging her into his war. The war was over now—or this one battle, anyway—but what would come of his renewing the acquaintance, playing on her gratitude that way?

"This whole thing makes me stop and think about the job," Carlisle said, sipping at his beer and staring into space. "It feels like ten years wasted, if you get my drift."

"Not wasted," Bolan said. "You make a difference every day you're on the street."

"You wouldn't know it, looking at the record. If I had a dime for every piece of shit who's walked on busts, no matter what I do, I could retire in style."

"You wouldn't, though."

"Don't be so sure."

"I'm sure enough," Bolan replied. "I can tell you weren't just looking for a pension when you took the job. I'd bet the farm that there are people still alive today because of you."

"Maybe. It's easier to count the dead ones, though."

"Tell me about it," Bolan said.

"I'll tell you one thing. I *liked* it. No rules, I mean. Go in and clean the bastards out like they were shit, and I'm the shovel. What's that tell you? I've been chasing them so long, I'm one of them."

"Not even close. Believe it. You don't have the smell."

"What smell is that?"

"The death smell. You're familiar with it, right?"

"I guess I am."

"There's not enough cologne on earth to cover it. You smell it coming off a predator, first time you meet him. That is, if you've got the nose for it."

"And if you don't?"

"You would have found yourself another business in the first place."

Carlisle checked his watch and finished off his beer. "I'd

better get down to the gate," he said. "Check-in and all."
He reached for Bolan's hand and shook it. "If it's all the same to you, I'll go alone."

"No sweat."

"It's been a slice."

"I'd say."

He stood and watched Tom Carlisle vanish into the crowd. There was a bank of public telephones outside the coffee shop. Bolan dropped a few coins in the slot and tapped out a number for New Orleans.

"Marianne? It's Mike Belasko.... No, I'm fine. The reason why I called... Tonight? Well, I don't... Are you sure that's such a good idea...? Well, if you're positive... Okay, then. All right, I'll see you in three or four hours."

He cradled the receiver, smiling, and walked the fifty yards back to the ticket counter.

"Yes, sir?" The woman was blond and perky, barely started on her shift.

"I need a ticket to New Orleans on your next flight out."

"Round trip?"

"One way," he said, and thought, Why not?

The war would still be waiting for him in a day or two.

Stony Man turns the tide of aggression against the world's most efficient crime machines

STONY MAN™ 32

LAW OF LAST RESORT

The playground of the Caribbean becomes a drug clearing house for an ex-KGB major and his well-oiled machine handling cocaine and heroin from the cartels and the Yakuza. But turquoise waters turn bloodred as Mack Bolan, Able Team and Phoenix Force deliver a hellfire sweep that pulls the CIA, international mafiosi and Colombians together in an explosive showdown.

Available in January 1998 at your favorite retail outlet.

James Axler

OUTLANDERS™

OMEGA PATH

A dark and unfathomable power governs post-nuclear America. As a former warrior of the secretive regime, Kane races to expose the blueprint of a power that's immeasurably evil, with the aid of fellow outcasts Brigid Baptiste and Grant. In a pre-apocalyptic New York City, hope lies in their ability to reach one young man who can perhaps alter the future....

Nothing is as it seems. Not even the invincible past....

Available February 1998,
wherever Gold Eagle books are sold.

A violent struggle for survival
in a post-holocaust world

JAMES AXLER

DEATH LANDS®

Nightmare Passage

Ryan Cawdor and his companions fear they have crossed time lines
when they encounter an aspiring god-king whose ambitions are
straight out of ancient Egypt. In the sands of California's Guadalupe
Desert, Ryan must make the right moves to save them from another
kind of hell—abject slavery.

**Don't miss out on the action in these titles
featuring THE EXECUTIONER®, STONY MAN™
and SUPERBOLAN®!**

GEBACK19